THE RISE OF THE DAGGER

What Happens in a Rugby Story When Life Interrupts?

A novel by Gcobani Bobo and Elvis Jack

COPYRIGHT

THE RISE OF THE DAGGER

Copyright © 2015 Gcobani Bobo and Elvis Jack.

Print ISBN: 978-0-620-66792-0

eBook ISBN 978-1-329-76146-9

First Edition: July 2015

Cover design by Christine Vaissiere

Layout, eBook conversion and distribution by www.bulabuka.co.za

TABLE OF CONTENTS

SYNOPSIS

Xolile Dalindyebo comes out of nowhere to play rugby explosively. He is from the Eastern Cape, speaks Xhosa and, mysteriously, Japanese. His history is uncertain but the fans love him because he is, in effect, a black Christian Cullen – small yet very strong, electrifyingly fast with an intelligent side step and an instinct for the game.

He forms a long term business arrangement with Allison Meyer, a divorcee in her forties and maverick journalist. Together they construct his public persona carefully using twitter and other social media both to project his image and to protect his past.

As his popularity increases his role within the team grows stronger and he assumes the captaincy after some inner club manoeuvring.

In parallel with this, Xolile embarks on a series of reconnaissance visits to unlikely places to recruit extra players, a bit like the search for special skills in the Magnificent Seven film. He eventually recruits six additional players. With extra talent and a slew of new tactics on the field, this could finally be the year of the Lions…

But nothing is as it seems in the world of rugby and Xolile's past may still return to haunt him and the team….

Gcobani Bobo played professional rugby for 15 years for a number of local and foreign teams, including the Springboks, the South African national side. He currently coaches and commentates on rugby.

Elvis Jack is the author of a number of books.

PART ONE

1

From The Citizen newspaper, 11th April 2014:

The Golden Lions narrowly won their match against the Argentinian Pampas XV on Saturday at Ellis Park by 35 points to 21. Star of the game was young debutant winger, Xolile Dalindyebo, who scored 4 tries, one of them a long-range effort from his own half. Dalindyebo is a new signing by the Lions who won only 3 games last season.

Mike Chisholm plumped himself down on the seat next to Willem Pretorius. Below them the grounds of the University of Johannesburg was crammed with rugby players - in front of them the forwards practiced line out drills, away in the distance the back line was attempting a complex double around maneuver.

"Mike."

"Willie."

The two men had worked together on and off for the past two years. Chisholm was a New Zealand born ex player turned coach. Bought at vast expense by the cash rich Johannesburg Super Rugby bosses in an attempt to boost the fortunes of the chronically underperforming Lions Super Rugby team, Mike Chisholm was regarded by some as the world's best coach. In his first year Willem had been his assistant coach. A grudging respect had grown between the two men. Willem liked Mike, thought he was smart even, but didn't share others' belief in his superhuman powers. For the past year Willem had coached the provincial Lions team that played in the local league. The money, though, was in the international Super 15 competition.

"I know why you here," Willem said to him.

"Yeah?"

"Your wing crisis. I suppose you're interested in Dalindyebo ...?"

"Four tries on debut - not many players do that. What do you think of him?"

"Not bad; he's got a bit of toe on him. Two of those tries I could have scored but one he carried three guys on his back to get to the line... and the fourth was a real beauty – from his own line cut left, cut right and when he seemed to have been stopped just exploded up the centre, beautifully done..."

Mike nodded, "Yeah, yeah, I saw the highlights package on TV. Can he tackle, catch the ball, kick? In short, Willie, do you think he's Super Rugby standard?"

Willie kicked at the bench in front of him as though he didn't want to commit to an answer. Far away the grunt as two scrums engaged was music to his ears. Finally he said:

"It's hard to be certain of his potential: pace - plenty, fields the high ball very well, tackles - pretty good... but I dunno..."

"Say it," said Mike encouragingly.

"He's got an attitude, a funny attitude... hard to describe... but if you're desperate, take him, I don't think he'll let you down..."

"What? Another strong silent sulky type? A steroid rager like that other lunatic you sent me?"

Willem laughed. "No, no, he won't try and hit you with a dustbin this one. And he's anything but silent, he'll talk the hind leg off a donkey. But he's an odd guy, that's all I'm saying. And he's got the weirdest tattoos on his back and chest – wait till you see him with his shirt off…"

"I don't care about his poncy body art. I just want him to put his body on the line for the team. Call him over, Willem."

Pretorius summoned one his hangers on a few metres away: "Jy, ja jy, gaan roep vir X, ja vir daai ou Dalindyebo ."

"X? What kind of a name is X?" Before Pretorius could answer Xolile Dalindyebo came loping over.

Chisholm's first thought was that he wasn't very big. If he had been expecting a giant, a Lomu or Rokococo bursting through tackles, this kid wasn't it. Dalindyebo wore dreadlocks and had a strange tail of a tattoo curling up through his training jersey collar before fading away at the angle of his jaw.

"Xolile, this is Mike Chisholm" said Pretorius by way of introduction.

Dalindyebo shook his hand "I know you of course, I've seen you on TV, Sir." His voice was soft, almost feminine.

"Don't call him sir. We're not in the British army here", said Pretorius. Mike cleared his throat to speak but Dalindyebo was too fast. "Good news for me perhaps?" he asked quickly.

"What makes you think that?"

"Well you are the Super 15 coach… I assume when I'm asked to meet you that there is some interest in me for the squad. But maybe I'm wrong – you must say."

"Yes, well you know, of course, that Van Staden's done his knee, out for the season, Craven is suspended for 4 weeks and now Pieterse's done a hamstring in training. We'd like you to join the squad, yes, just as backup at first."

Chisholm realized that somehow the advantage was not with him anymore. "Can you…" he started to say but Dalindyebo cut in "I'd love to do that, really, it would be a dream come true for me."

Chisholm was frankly irritated now: "Can you take the high ball all right?"

Dalindyebo nodded enthusiastically. "Yes, you know I spent a year in Melbourne playing Aussie Rules, only second league you understand, but the training is very strong on catching the ball in the air. So I'm fine with that."

"What about kicking? Any good at that?" barked Chisholm.

"Ah, Coach… Ok if I call you that? That's a real weak point of mine. I practiced it during the Aussie rules time in Melbourne but not enough - but I'm working on that part of my game."

"You can't run every ball back, not at Super Rugby level any way. A good fullback needs to be able to kick sometimes."

"I know, Coach, I'm putting in a lot of hours trying to improve, as I said". Dalindyebo was smiling now, genuinely pleased it seemed that he was being interviewed as a team member.

"Willem says you've got some pace. You play center or wing ever?"

"Fullback is my position. I've played wing sometimes but it's not my favourite. Centre, I can't play center, I'm just no good for that, too physical for me maybe…"

"We need a player who'll fulfill whatever role is good for the team. If I ask you to play center I expect you to do so." Chisholm had had enough of this kid and he had only just met him, he was later to say to Pretorius.

"No, no, Coach, don't misunderstand me: I'll play anywhere, do anything for the team, but I'm just no damn good at center…." His grin was wider now.

"Well, anyway we'll see how you go. Report tomorrow at our training ground at Ellis Park at 10; go and see Mrs Arendse at the Lions office before and she'll give you the standard 3 match contract. We'll see after that if we still need you or whether you'll go back to the Willlem's team."

2

"Thabo.....!"

"I know, I know...."

Thabo Motsepe sprang from his desk mumbling "nagging bitch" under his breath. The newsroom was almost deserted. He strolled around looking for someone to pass his problem onto. He turned into the sports alcove and greeted the sports editor.

"John" he said to John Macintyre, "how's it going, man?"

John looked at him over his spectacles. "And our news department wants what exactly?"

Thabo plopped down on the seat next to his desk.

"A simple request, John. My old school friend, Keith Meyer, divorced his wife, Allison, recently. She's taken it badly... She's got a journalism degree from Rhodes but never worked, raised two babies until a few months ago. I agreed to her attachment to me for a few months, unpaid of course...."

"Wanting what from me, exactly?"

"Do you have a project for her to work on? She's smart, a serious person, she can do almost any topic..."

John waved him away irritably and grabbed a piece of paper off his desk. "Here, let her interview this guy: Xolile Dalindyebo just came out of nowhere, scored a bunch of tries for the provincial team. Now they say he's going to play for the Lions Super Rugby franchise. No one knows where he's from. She can interview him for ten pages, maybe we'll run a paragraph next week."

"Thanks man, John...."

Back to his office. "ALLISON" he bellowed, "I have something for you...."

3

Xolile looked at himself in the mirror of his little bathroom. He greeted his image with an air punch.

"Yes!" he said in self congratulation.

His cell phone rang.

"Dalindyebo" he said into the phone.

"Hi, is that Xolile Dalindyebo? My name is Allison Meyer. I work for The Star. We'd like to do an article on you for the sports pages..."

4

The team biokineticist, Jeremy, called Mike Chisholm over at the gym.

"The new guy, Xolile, he's physically an impressive specimen," said Jeremy.

"Yeah, how so?"

"For a start he's really quick over 40 metres – 4.6 seconds, easily the fastest we've seen this year."

"Well, we knew that from his provincial games…"

"But what's most impressive is his strength. You remember we record the proportion of body weight each player can lift in bench press?"

"You know I don't really understand this conditioning technical stuff," Chisholm was gazing in to the middle distance, not really paying attention, "so you better tell me all that again."

"Well it's quite simple. One would expect a prop forward weighing 130 kg to press a much larger weight than a wing weighing 90 kg. But Xolile can press almost 220 kg – that's about 270 % of his body weight."

"Is that good?"

"It's the best in the squad."

"Well I'm not impressed. There's more to being a great rugby player than being fast and strong." Mike wandered off to speak to the forwards coach.

"But surely it's a good start" Jeremy mumbled to himself and the coach's back.

5

Allison sat on the stoep of Ninos in Rosebank. She was early and anxious. She realized that she had no idea what he looked like. She had Googled his name that morning. The only Google entry was a 12 year old in New Zealand who could do long division in his head. She assumed he would be a large man, maybe with those funny scarred ears rugby players sometimes had? She wiped her hands on her skirt, fiddled with her hair.

"Allison? Xolile Dalindyebo."

He was much smaller than she expected, casually dressed in jeans and loose fitting long sleeved T shirt. He had mid length dread locks and an odd looking tattoo crept out of his shirt collar and caressed the angle of his jaw. They shook hands formally and he sat opposite her. They both ordered cappuccinos.

Allison switched on her lap top, opened her mouth to speak.

"How long have you been a journalist?" he asked.

"I graduated 10 years ago."

"What have you written recently?"

"Oh, lots of things... Though sport is new for me. I don't know much about rugby, I have to admit."

"What things have you written?" Damn him, she thought, who's in charge here anyway.

"Let's get back to you..."

"No, sorry, I want to be clear. What have you had published before?"

He stared at her fixedly. Suddenly she was uncontained. "Ok, ok ... I've never had a thing in print. I'm a newly divorced trained journalist with no experience. My life is shit and you are my first and maybe my last interview. Are you satisfied now?"

He smiled at her for the first time. "Perfect" he said. "Let's order something to eat."

Allison felt somewhat more at ease when they ordered toasted sandwiches.

"Look", she said to him in an attempt to ingratiate, "Research!" She plonked a fat manila folder of Internet printouts down on the table. "I knew nothing about rugby before I was given this assignment, I've read all these pages and I still know nothing…"

He laughed at her. "Here's a potted summary of rugby: it's a contact sport where the aim is to dot the ball down on the opposing team's tryline which is at the end of the field near the toilets and the beer tents. To do that a team has only two options of getting there – to kick the ball or to run with the ball. And because it's a contact sport it's seldom possible simply to run the ball from one side to another – players will tackle you to stop you – and so you need to be able to pass to another player to take the ball up. When the ball is stopped in play it needs a special set of players to restart it: if it's a scrum you need short fat strong men; if it's a lineout you need tall thin men; and if it's a kick you need players who can kick far and accurately…" He paused and smiled again "and that's rugby …"

He attacked his toasted sandwich as she paged through her file of printouts trying to marry what he had said to what others had.

"And which are you?" she asked.

"I'm what is sometimes known as a finisher. I am a fullback who can run fast and when there's a hole in the defense, usually created by the rest of the team hammering the opponents so that the team is in a superior position, my job is to take the ball and score the try. Finishers are usually wings but we can be also be fullbacks..."

"So you are the star of the team?"

"No, the forwards who grind the opponents down are the stars. But sometimes we finishers do things that look spectacular so the newspapers like us 'cos we make good photos and stories for them. That's why your boss told you to interview me."

She flipped open her notebook and said: "Tell me about yourself."

"No" he said.

"What?"

"We're in negotiation about our roles first. Here's the truth: I am currently a nobody – your readers have never heard of me. But I have just been promoted to a team that plays internationally against other teams like ourselves from New Zealand and Australia. And maybe, if I am right and I am good enough, I am about to become a household name. Your newspaper got it wrong – I am not an 'up and coming youngster', I am 27 years old and I've done lots of things in the past. Some of those things I don't want to talk about in public, I'm a private person really."

He was silent for a while.

"So what are we negotiating then?" she asked him.

"Given my current status, you'd be lucky to get a paragraph in print about me. But if I do well in the coming weeks you might well find that your bosses will run a much longer feature on me. I'll work closely with you on both pieces so that your first printed articles will be exclusive and mildly interesting. In return I want editing rights on what you write…"

"But that's unethical!" she exclaimed.

"How so?" Again that impish grin of his.

"You will in effect be writing an article about yourself and we'll publish it as though it's an objective account. That's completely immoral for a newspaper."

"Oh come on. I'm not Bernie Madoff or Klaus Barbie – I'm a professional sportsman. What can it possibly matter if I write my own story? And, anyway, I'm not asking to write it merely to remove bits I don't like. Plus, just to sweeten the pot, if I really become famous you'll get exclusive rights to my interviews with the Argus group of newspapers; and I'll recommend you to other rugby players who need interviewing. This could be the start of a new career for you."

Allison sipped her coffee, munched on her sandwich for a long time.

"Are you hustling me?"

He burst out laughing and prodded her arm conspiratorially; after a moment she joined him and they giggled together like old friends.

"I'm going to take that as a yes, we have a deal, right?" he said.

"Let's take it as a try and see where we go from here. But tell me, off the record, what are the things in your past that you want to hide?"

"I might tell you one day but not on the first meeting; I hardly know you after all.... Incidentally, I think I get free tickets for a box at Ellis Park if I play Super 15. You can have the tickets if you want, see your first rugby game. We play the Blues, a pretty good team."

6

Alison sat in the box above the half way line. She had had two brandy and cokes forced on her by a large man called Rudi whose son played scrumhalf for the Lions and her head was spinning both from the alcohol and the occasion. Several things had surprised her: it was late evening on an autumn Highveld day and the dark had fallen quickly. The flood lights were on they were simply spectacular: the field and the stadium were light as a summer's day. She could see the players clearly, even their facial expressions. The crowd was loud but not raucous and only slightly drunk as a group. There was an air of excitement that she found infectious, attractive even.

She had been shocked at the sheer violence of the tackles. Nothing she'd seen on TV had prepared her for grunts of effort and pain, the impact of body on body – was this really a sport, she pondered to herself or men using sport as an excuse to fight each other?

Rudi had been helpful once she told him truthfully how little she knew about the game and her interest in Xolile Dalindyebo for her newspaper. He had pointed out each time Dalindyebo had touched the ball and assured her at half time that he was doing well – put in three solid tackles and claimed a high ball twice with great confidence. She hadn't seen him run yet but Rudi told her that people said he had "some gas" on him.

The game continued. Allison could imagine how people could be absorbed, fascinated, obsessed even, with rugby – but it wasn't for her, she was fairly sure. Watching her first game, though, she had to admit she was surprised about certain things. Having watched excerpts only previously she had always thought it was like that village in Wales that as a tourist attraction had a once a year game where the locals wrestled through the mud for a day in search of a pigs bladder or something. In fact, rugby union was nothing like that – much of the game was static with players lined up against each other in set formations. It was a stylized brutality, she said to herself, interrupted occasionally by some spectacular individual or collective bits of style and grace...

Five minutes to go and the Lions were trailing by 24 points to 18. On the halfway line the Lions moved the ball down the backline ("Bout time" grunted Rudi) and suddenly between two players (the centres Rudi told her later) Xolile popped up, was passed the ball and took off.

Once again Allison was surprised: Xolile had told her he was fast, was very good at certain aspects of the game, and who was she to doubt the truth of his boasts? But nothing had prepared her for the grace and power of him on the run.

Everyone in the box was on their feet, many shouting. She rose too, the better to watch Xolile take off like a, like a bullet, like an arrow from a bow, in her own mind she shuffled through clichés to describe him. Forty metres from the tryline he headed for the corner, his peculiar high kicking stride eating up the distance. The last player, the opposing fullback, came running across to cut him off – surely he would bring him down or was Xolile strong enough to knock him over?

In the event neither happened as the two players converged Xolile kicked somehow so that without breaking stride where he was running to the left he was now running towards the right hand corner. The opposing fullback carried on heading to Xolile's left and it was all over. Without a hand being laid on him Xolile dotted the ball down under the posts. He did it with the same lack of flamboyance that was to mark all his tries. He simply dotted the ball down and carried it back with him towards the half way line without celebration.

Rudi slapped her on the shoulder none too gently. "Beautiful, classical," he told her. He then explained to her about the split between the centres. "If he goes fast enough there is no one marking him, just the cover defence coming across and the fullback defending at the back... and then that sidestep – fantastic, straight out of the manuals..."

But wait something seemed to be going on, there were replays, boos rang out from the fans, Rudi was muttering "No, no man".

"What's going on?" she asked him.

"I dunno" he said, "I think the fucking ref is screwing us again. . . Look there it is on the big screen."

Sure enough in a replay on the giant screen she could see a fist come out of nowhere and hit the player in blue in the face. The crowd was booing loudly and a few naatjies were being hurled on to the field.

"But surely that happened before, it had nothing to do with the try?" she said to Rudi.

He looked at her with a new respect: "Exactly!"

This was Allison's first exposure to a phenomenon she would see again and again in the coming years: for South African fans, often the most generous in acknowledging the achievements of their opponents, the referees were always against them. Whether this was part of an anti-Afrikaans bias or whether they resented us because we had better weather than them, this remained the most ubiquitous of myths amongst local fans.

The try was disallowed, a Lions player sent off for punching, the Blues kicked a penalty and the game was lost. Allison looked at Xolile's face through binoculars during the whole episode. He appeared unfazed largely, certainly much less perturbed than Rudi, with an almost smile playing about his lips.

More alcohol was dispensed from somewhere in the box. Word had spread that she was interested in the star of the moment. A large man handed her a rum and coke and lectured her on the sidestep versus the swerve (or what he called a "jink").

As she was leaving Xolile sent her an sms suggesting they meet at his apartment. Allison had only a moment's pause about meeting a relatively unknown black man at his inner city flat.

After all, she told herself, newly divorced, no sex for six months, what was the worst that could possibly happen by being alone with a handsome young man in his twenties?

7

Xolile's apartment was rather lovely she thought. Perched on top of a renovated building in Noord Street in the city he had joined two little flats to make a loft style 150 square metre living area with a sumptuous view of the lights of Berea in the distance. A circular metal staircase lead to a roof garden, done Japnanese style with raked stones in an obsessively neat pattern and little plants growing in aisles alongside.

"Nice place" she said as he poured a little saki. "You own it?"

"Yes, I came back from Japan with a bit of money. In Japan you would have to be extremely rich to afford a place of this size for one person. Make yourself at home, I'm just popping into the shower then we'll write your piece for The Star, right?"

She wandered around his apartment picking up little Japanese gewgaws, tea sets, miniature stone gardens with little rakes and plants... His book shelf was almost empty except for two books in Japanese – it took her a long while to realize one was a version of Sun Tzu's Art of War.

Xolile came back in a towel and simply took her breath away. He had the most perfect body she had ever seen on a man – chiselled, toned, it seemed to her that every muscle in his body stood ready for action.

"Let's see that tattoo" she said to cover her discomfort. He turned around and she saw the tattoo starting just above his buttocks as a dragon, then swirling across his back before emerging as two roses over his shoulders and ending in a wisp around his neck.

"Beautiful" she said, "Where did you get it?"

"I had a friend who was a real artist with a needle; took about two months to finish."

"And the bruises?" Across his caramel coloured torso a chain of bruises could be seen on his back with one huge one on his upper chest.

"What bruises?" He looked in the hall mirror "Oh these, no these are standard rugby stuff. It happens pretty much after every big game…"

He came out of his bedroom wearing an old track suit and made tea for both of them – Japanese style of course, heavy on style and low on taste, Allison thought to herself.

"So are you pleased with the way things worked out in the game?" she asked him.

"Overall, very pleased. You know I believed I could play, succeed even at this level, but I still worried that I might be deceiving myself – that when I played against really good players I might be a nothing, a tote along that contributes nothing to the team. Now I know. I can play much better than I did today, I was just trying to be an old style fullback to impress the coach."

Allison sipped her tea. "You know when you left the field after the match some of the kids were chanting your name…."

"Ja, that was sort of cool, I suppose."

"I think you need a twitter account - and a facebook page."

He thought for a moment. "I'm a bit out of touch with these things… Tell me what the advantage would be for me?"

"Well it would be a way of being in touch with your fan base, of increasing the size of it, expressing opinions that you wouldn't want to make in an interview – things like that."

"You know about things like this?"

Allison was suddenly struck by diffidence: "I did my Masters on it – the confluence of social media and journalism."

"Yeah? What else could we do with it?" He seemed to have switched a mental gear.

Allison spoke for some time on the potential for a new celebrity to interact with fans. He seemed to drink this all in. She noticed he was fiddling with a little toy or ornament, another Japanese thing.

"What is that thing?"

"Oh it's a Netsuku, a Japanese cultural whatsit, part good luck charm, part miniature art. Look, it has a rugby motif. It was another gift from Yukio, my tattoo artist."

He passed it on to Allison who was surprised by the weight. It was cool to the touch, made of jade perhaps, and was a tiny sculpture of a fat man with a rugby ball clasped to his stomach.

The hour was late and Allison made ready to leave. Suddenly there was a silence between them, almost awkward. A dozen thoughts swirled in Allison's head. When she spoke it was almost as if the previous thoughts had been said aloud.

"This is business. It's important to both of us..."

And amazingly, she thought later, Xolile seemed to have followed her thoughts quite closely. "Absolutely," he said, "business comes first. We'll meet very soon."

And she left. Something had been agreed to, she thought, but she wasn't sure if she were pleased or regretful about it...

8

From The Star newspaper April 16th 2014:

Xolile Dalindyebo, exciting new prospect at fullback for the Lions, says playing for the Lions has always been a dream of his since his childhood in the Transkei. "Playing for them was probably the best day of my life" he said excitedly after the match. His only current ambition he says is to secure his place in the team. Xolile, who despite his youthful looks, is 27, admits to being a bit of a rolling stone in previous years – he played in Japan for several seasons and spent a bit of time playing Aussie Rules football for the Footscray team in Melbourne, mainly to hone his skills at taking the high ball. "But no longer" he says, "I want to make Johannesburg, and the Lions, my home."

Allison and Xolile were sitting in a posh Rosebank Japanese restaurant, eating some frighteningly expensive Japanese dish with deep fried vegetables and sea food.

"Never mind the money" he told her as they sat down, "It's in the form of a celebration – things are going according to plan, more or less…" To add to her mixed feelings he then ordered the food in perfect Japanese.

"What plan?" she said, "are there things you are not telling me?"

"Of course" he said brusquely, "show us the article".

"Reads well," Xolile said, handing the newspaper back to Allison.

"I'm not surprised you like it seeing as how you wrote it". Allison surprised herself with her waspish tone.

"I wrote it – nah, look it says at the top there, by Allison Meyer. And if I'm not mistaken isn't that the first byline by Allison Meyer, soon to be the doyenne of rugby journalists?"

"And here's your first draft tweet. I've trawled a lot of rugby players' tweets and they all seem terrifically sweet and generous. So I took the liberty of saying this: *great to be part of the team terrific bunch of guys hope I can do well* .What do you think? It's not sent yet you just to have to edit it and press here."

"I don't ever want to use the word 'guys', no matter what the circumstances are," he said after a while, "and I want to appear to be humble about my future in the team... how about simply *"great team, great stadium, great atmosphere ... I wish I could be part of it for years to come."*

He paused again. "Bit boring though isn't it?"

"Perfect for a start – you can't be bold until you have an audience... "

"How do I get an audience again?"

"Keep scoring tries – isn't that your job?"

"That's my job OK" he said with a cocky grin. "We're on tour next week for the month – Perth, Christchurch, Sydney and Otago. We'll keep in touch by email, yes?"

"And Skype of course, I'll show you how...." Allison suddenly realized she would miss him, this mysterious man with the tattoo.

"I'm taking a liking to this twitter stuff" he said, picking up some rice with his chopsticks, "I've got a great one for when we play The Crusaders in three weeks. It's going to really stick it to them..."

"Then that's what your next tweet should be," she said.

"What?"

"In my next tweet I'm going to stick it to the Crusaders – it builds an interest, a following."

"Maybe…" he said.

"Look, Xolile, this is fun for me I have to admit, learning a bit about rugby, getting little things in the newspaper… but what is my role in the future? You talk of plans but you don't share them with me. What will happen when you are an established player? What's in it for me?"

He thought for a while as they munched on exquisite bits of crackling food. "Allison, my goal is simple: in the next two years I plan on captaining the Lions, turning them into a winning exciting team and then do the same for the national side. All interviews in the future will go through you. I hope in time you'll be my sort of PR person, manager, business manager, a whole series of roles in one. Nothing fancy – one step at a time…"

"You intend being Springbok captain?" It was the first time she had heard him say it.

"Sure; it's the goal of every rugby player in the country, even schoolboys – nothing unusual in that."

"I read on the internet that Dan Carter has a permanent contract advertising men's underwear". She remembered the vision of him in a towel the previous week.

"See: I knew you'd have ideas. Arrange something like that and you can take a fee as well."

He was silent for a moment. "And while I'm in Australasia you could write other things for your newspaper. You could do, say, a page on the dummy or the scissors – all these old rugby techniques. They have a rich history probably – a bit of research on the internet you could do that. Being new to rugby would be an advantage, bring a fresh insight from someone who's never played the game."

"Maybe... I'll think about it."

Following the Blues match, The Citizen newspaper rugby correspondent, the well-respected Tsidi Montoedi, wrote a review of the match concentrating on Xolile and his future.

Quite simply he compared him to Christian Cullen, the iconic New Zealand full back who had retired four or five years previously. He pointed out the fact that he claimed had escaped other commentators, that the two players were remarkably similar.

He highlighted the pace, similar confidence, similar high kicking electrifying running and acceleration, even a similar ability to make the players around him seem better than they were when he wasn't playing.

He ended with the words: *And just as in New Zealand for almost a decade all attacks were built around the unique abilities of Christian Cullen, so too in South Africa at national and provincial level we should prepare ourselves for the Dalindyebo era.*

"You paid this guy off to write this, didn't you?" Mike Chisholm said waving the article around.

"Didn't need to because Tsidi Montoedi is me; it's one of my pseudonyms," Xolile replied. He thought to himself that humble wasn't doing it with the coach – perhaps he should try cocky for a while.

"That's not true – he interviewed me last year, he's a real person....
Oh ok, I took you seriously for a moment," said Chisholm.

Various players tried out a nickname from the article. 'Christian' was
rejected predictably by the religious ("Particularly wrong for someone
who isn't" said Jacque the captain). He liked 'Blackullen' but no one
could quite pronounce it.

Eventually it was decided that his nickname would emerge at the
right time....

9

On the long plane ride to Australia Xolile didn't sleep. Instead he worked the team. Every person who had a light on was a target. He would sit down, chat a bit, look for common ground or not. In the twelve hour flight he managed to connect with almost every player.

He spent some time with Jacque De Villiers, the long standing lock and usual captain. Jacques told him that there was always shit going on at the Lions and he had a contract with Bath for next season. "Maybe if my body lasts I can do three seasons in England, come home with a bit of money, buy a business…"

Xolile asked him if he had any ideas about his replacement as number 4 lock next season. "There a couple of twenty year olds playing some games for the provincial team – they'll be ready in a year or two to step up. Otherwise I'm not sure who could take over."

Karel Buys told him of his plans to make the world cup squad in the following year. Xolile told him he thought he had a good chance, only a little white lie, he told himself.

The best for him was Jan Cilliers, a flank and some time captain. He discovered that Jan had a hobby, inherited from his father. He restored vintage English motor cycles. He was currently working on an Ariel Square Four that he had bought from a farmer in Ermelo the previous year. Jan was even more delighted to find that Xolile had worked for 6 months at a motorcycle repair shop in Melbourne and, holy of holies, had even seen two Ariels awaiting restoration at the back. Jan immediately wanted to head for Melbourne – he was desperate, he said, for a timing chain. He seemed vague about the distance from Perth to Melbourne. "It's like wanting a part in Cape

Town when you're in Joburg," Xolile told him.

Pleased with himself, Xolile suffered through the long video session when they landed. It was designed to keep the players awake so they could become local time orientated and recover as fast as possible from the crippling jet lag flying longitudinally across the globe. It was only at lunch time in Perth that he was finally able to catch his first sleep for 36 hours.

He shared a room at the hotel with Andile Phike, also a native Xhosa speaker.

"Welcome to the Black room" he said to Xolile by way of introduction. Xolile thought that Andile, the only other black (as opposed to coloured) player in the team was a good one – a hooker now in his early thirties who got better every year. He was now fitter, larger and more dependable than he had been five years previously when he occupied the Springbok reserve bench with little game time. They chatted away in Xhosa through the night.

Xolile tweeted before the game: *Perth – nice weather it's like Bloemfontein with a beach*

Number of followers: 137.

Allison settled down to watch the match at home with her daughters, Leah and Rosemary.

"Which one is your crush, Mum?" said 17 year old Rosemary.

"He's not my crush, he's my job" said Allison, "there he is at the back with 15 on his jersey and the dreadlocks."

With Allison having watched one more game of rugby than her

daughters, plus sundry readings on the internet, she was able to give them a kind of running commentary on the set pieces, the drives and the occasional spectacular move.

In fact, the game was a sparkling one for the Lions. With sunny weather and a sizable local support from ex South Africans in Perth they produced a complete performance. They ran in five tries to two and won by 41 points to 12.

Xolile did not score any tries but had a hand in at least 3 of them, earning himself the man of the match award. Every time he touched the ball all three women gave a little shriek – a kind of there-he-goes signal… and Xolile touched the ball a lot. He did his fullback job of last defence and fielding the high kicks proficiently, he ran, he linked, he created gaps and eventually tries.

Allison was only partly satisfied. "He's the finisher – he should be scoring the tries," she told her daughters.

In the post-match interview Xolile was gracious. He praised the field and their opponents and the crowd. "There seemed to be a lot of support for the Lions in Perth" remarked the interviewer.

"Ja," said Xolile, "We hope in future we'll be the favourite amongst the locals, after their own team of course. And we hope we'll be favourites because of our type of rugby rather than where we're from…"

The interviewer began to turn away but Xolile stopped him. "Do you mind if I say something to the folks back home in my own language?"

"Certainly" said the interviewer, only slightly bemused.

Xolile then said in Xhosa: *Bantu bakuthi ukuba anisixhasi nokuba nenza impazamo.*

Which Allison later found out translated roughly into: you black people at home if you support any other team rather than the Lions you are making a big mistake.

She logged into his twitter account just before she went to bed that night. He had written: *good game for us. Crusaders supporters watch this space: I have a dagger for your hearts*

Followers: 576

And on Sunday, just after the team landed in Christchurch, he tweeted: *Crusaders terrific team for years but whats with the Crusades? Celebrating looting and massacres?*

Followers 2,315

On his facebook page he made a link to a Wikipedia article on The Crusades and ended with a quote from a French historian who had witnessed the massacre of Jerusalem in the 11th century:

... Wonderful sights were to be seen. Some of our men (and this was more merciful) cut off the heads of their enemies; others shot them with arrows, so that they fell from the towers; others tortured them longer by casting them into the flames. Piles of heads, hands and feet were to be seen in the streets of the city. It was necessary to pick one's way over the bodies of men and horses. But these were small matters compared to what happened at the Temple of Solomon, a place where religious services are normally chanted ... in the temple and the porch of Solomon, men rode in blood up to their knees and bridle reins. Indeed it was a just and splendid judgment of God that this place should be filled with the blood of unbelievers since it had suffered so long from their blasphemies.

Raymond D'Aguilers in *Historia Francorum qui ceperunt Iherusalem*

And he tweeted *what do Sonny Billy and Jacob say about this?*

Followers: 5,355

On Tuesday of that week the Crusaders Social Media Team took the unusual step of responding to a tweet. They issued a lengthy statement itemizing the team's long and glorious history and called the Crusades irrelevant to the current team.

On Wednesday Xolile tweeted: *Irrelevant? Then why do we have horses and a castle at the ground? And what's with all that sword play?*

Followers: 9, 333

Christchurch on Saturday wasn't just freezing cold. The wind howled off the River Avon close by and little needles of icy rain stung one's face in the city. The small ground was nearly full though. "There's fuck all else to do in this town except play or watch rugby" said Andile.

Mike Chisholm walked through the crowd and came back livid.

"Dalindyebo, what is this crap you've been writing on your facebook page? Do you know the whole crowd is made up with black boot polish or something; they're all dressed in black and there are signs saying 'Kill the dagger' and 'Dalindyebo shit'. They're baying for our blood out there…"

"Doesn't seem any different to other times we've played here" muttered Jacques De Villiers.

"It bloody well is! The crowd is fired up, The Crusaders will be fired up and it's all your doing, Dalindyebo. Take this as your last warning: shut the fuck up about everything in future."

Xolile muttered a few words of apology to the team. "I hadn't realized they would take such offence to an offhand remark..."

Allison watched the game at home again. This time her sister Angela with husband Mitch joined the two girls and her. The game was a brutal forward battle in driving icy rain. The field was a mud bath. Every time Xolile touched the ball the stadium resounded with boos and the fans shook their 'Kill the Dagger' posters to try and catch the TV cameras.

Mike observed that the conditions might actually favour the Lions in that the Crusaders couldn't run them off their feet like they usually did.

10

I glanced at the clock – 34 minutes in the first half gone. I was standing on our 22 metre line, the play was on the half way, close to the touch line. The Crusaders were in possession and I was expecting a kick. I moved a few metres closer to the left in case it was a cross kick. The temperature with the cruel wind chill factor must have been close to zero but, although I was soaking wet, I wasn't cold – a few recent tackles and runs had seen to that for the moment.

The ball came out and the Crusaders right wing made a ten metre run down the touchline. Still I was expecting a kick but I moved closer to the right – a left headed kick was less likely now. The wing was held up but popped a lovely pass in the tackle to their eighth man and he pelted down the touchline. I knew he wasn't a kicker but only I stood between him and the goal line. Time to go now....

I launched myself at him, leading with my shoulder, holding my breath. At the moment of impact I tucked my head in for protection, my shoulder aiming at his elbow attached to the arm attached to the ball. We hit only two metres or so from the touchline and my impetus took us both over the line in a heap – our throw in. The number eight rose by pressing his big forearm into my throat as he levered himself upright.

"Go back to where you come from, Nigger" he hissed at me.

I sprang up and followed his back as he made to trot back into position. "Is that all you've got? What do you think you are a redneck from the fifties? Nobody uses the word 'nigger' anymore. What a moron you must be... what a halfwit...."

He turned back to me, his arms upraised in innocence. "What did I do?" he said.

"You're an idiot" I told him, "where I come from they call us kaffirs, not niggers, you can't even get your insults right…"

Other players pulled us apart.

"Trouble?" asked Jan solicitously.

"No, nothing" I said, rubbing my throat as I walked back to my position. I glanced again at the clock. Thirty five minutes gone – another minute of Super Rugby had passed.

11

At half time the score was 12 to the Crusaders 6 to the Lions, all penalties. Even the kickers struggled in the wind – in all there had been ten attempts at goal with only 6 successes.

As the Lions trudged in to the change room, Jeremy, the biokinetecist, distributed fresh warm and dry jerseys to each player. Some players had to run a shower over their heads to get the mud off before pulling the warm jerseys on.

"I think I'll stay here for an hour or two" said Jan Cilliers.

Mike Chisholm pulled no punches. "Stay with the game plan. Kick into their half and let them make the running… then tackle, tackle, tackle."

Xolile thought this was the wrong game plan. He thought the team needed to hold on to the ball, not kick it away, but this did not seem the time to mention it.

The coach caught his eye. "You! What have you got to say now Mr Bigmouth?"

"I say we should use the hatred of the crowd, soak it in, let the curses and the shouts be a motivation for us, become…"

"Shut the fuck up!" screamed Mike Chisholm.'

"I thought he asked me to speak" said Xolile to Andile as they trudged back out.

"I think that was a rhetorical question when he asked you what you had to say," said Andile as they reentered the storm chuckling.

As they went back on to the field Jan called the players into a huddle. "It's always like this when we play here – the fans are relentless in talking shit to us. Xolile say a few words to the guys."

Xolile was touched by Jan's sensitivity. "Remember how at school you knew in your heart you had a talent but no one realised how good you were. Like these Crusader fans who underestimate us, they look at our record, they think we are useless, they think we are no one special. But you know that we are special. They are scoffing at us. The Crusaders treat us like slaves of old, like the inhabitants of Jerusalem. THE TIME HAS COME TO RISE UP. Let's do it."

Nods and grunts and slapped palms followed and the team hurled themselves back into the fray.

Back in the Meyer house the girls were complaining that the game was dull compared to the previous week.

"It's dull but tense," said Allison, "see how quickly you can become an expert, a know it all, at rugby watching – it's only your second game."

On the field the war of attrition continued. Somehow a combination of determined defence by the Lions and a string of last passes going astray for the Crusaders led to no further score. With a half hour to play Chisholm brought on the reserve players. One forward drive and maul followed the next. The icy sheets of wind and rain made kicking for posts a poor alternative. Jan was replaced, exhausted, twenty minutes from the end and, almost unnoticed, Xolile assumed the captaincy for the first time. Allison watched him moving from player to player during stoppages, here a few words, there a clap on the shoulder.

"He should be captain" she told the others loyally.

It was still 12 points to 6 as the last 5 minutes of the game dawned. The Crusaders players were massed 5 metres from the Lions try line as the two sets of forwards hurled themselves at each other.

Suddenly the ball popped out and the Crusaders flyhalf shovelled the ball on to the big Crusaders wing, a Fijian with an unpronounceable surname the South Africans called "Tani" because that was the first syllable. The wing went for the left corner flag and it seemed that he must score when Xolile tackled him just a metre from the corner. It took a crunching collision to bring the bigger man down, bigger in fact by nearly 25 kilograms, and for a second both players lay in a heap. Tani pushed the ball back towards his own players. Xolile sprang up, stepped over him and plucked the ball from his fingers. Two Crusaders flanks rushed up to tackle him. They went in high aiming to push him over the touch line for a Crusaders throw in. For a moment all three players were in a tangle. Then Xolile emerged below the grasping arms of the forwards. They plucked at his muddy jersey but couldn't get a decent hold. And then he was away. He cut right across the field, saw a gap between the centres and went through it with his high kicking running style eating up the ground. And suddenly he was in the open, almost clear.

The crowd went silent as Xolile and the Crusaders fullback converged just outside the home team's 22 metre line. Xolile went for the right hand corner. "There's no space, he can't make it. Kick ahead, man" yelled Mitch back in Johannesburg.

But there was space after all. "There go the afterburners!" shouted the New Zealand commentator as Xolile went around the current All Black full back with some ease. He strolled in to the Crusaders try line but waited until the defenders arrived before dotting the ball down underneath the post.

Allison and her family were whooping with delight in her little lounge. Two minutes to go. As the kicker lined up the conversion Xolile trotted back to his position with a howl of boos greeting him from the crowd.

And then a strange thing happened: among the jeers and catcalls some of the crowd began to applaud the try. The clapping grew until it outweighed the boos. Xolile acknowledged the crowd with a grin and a slow rotation of an imaginary sword above his head. The jeers swelled again momentarily but now there was laughter as well. And then the chant began, low key at first but then swelling with each passing moment: "Dagger! Dagger! Dagger!..."

And that's how Xolile finally got his nickname....

The Lions, still down 12 to 11 needed the conversion to win – no formality in the gale. As the final whistle blew, the Lions flyhalf, Karel Buys, sent a wobbly kick sliding over the cross bar. The Lions had won.

Xolile was man of the match for the second week in succession.

"I don't deserve this one" he said in the post-match interview, "it should really go to a forward or two – they won the game for us."

"You came into this game with plenty of controversy but you seemed to fix it with the crowd at the end," said the interviewer.

"Well, we all know New Zealand crowds – they are passionate about their teams but always sporting to opponents."

Without asking this time he shifted into Xhosa for the fans at home.

As Mitch left Allison he said: "Sign this guy up, become his manager… there's money to be made here, don't let someone else steal him away."

12

Xolile and Allison spoke on Skype just before the Lions post match celebrations began.

"That was a great victory - and a great try", Allison told him.

"Thanks; this is, I think, a turning point for the team. To win a game we should have lost, a game that almost every other team in the world would have lost - we're ready for big things now."

"And this evening? Big celebration, I guess? Is that what you guys do after a victory?"

"You know I haven't experienced that many victories with this team but I'd guess this will be a big blow out. I'll have to get drunk with the lads; don't expect to hear from me for a couple of days - drinking is not really part of my skill set..."

They laughed and rang off, both of them aware of the warmth of their interaction.

But alcohol was to be a major part of the night - and the week that followed, a week the players were to christen Scandal Week.

Jeremy the biokinetecist had thoughtfully booked a distant relative's bar for the evening so the team was able to get completely smashed with only a handful of selected guests present.

What followed in the first part of the evening was somewhat juvenile. There were drunken, often sentimental speeches, weak skits and a general overload of sexual innuendo.

Jacques De Villiers thanked the team for their efforts on the field, which he seemed to believe were a tribute to himself. He finally went public with his plans for playing overseas - an event he believed no one knew about although having taken selected players into his confidence in the past weeks it was stale news to everyone.

Xolile saw Mike Chisholm head out some time around midnight and he took the opportunity to do his impression of him. Sporting quite a reasonable New Zealand accent, he replayed Chisholm's "What you got to say for yourself, Dalindyebo", followed by "I said shut the fuck up". He finished with one of Chisholm's trade mark sayings: "There's only one prick in this team and it's me, got it?"

The rest of the team, alcohol inspired, found it the funniest things they had ever heard.

At one in the morning the bar announced closing time. Some of the team headed for their hotels, some staggered out into the chill night air, too wound up to sleep, looking for more alcohol or women... Or a fight.

The three incidents that followed took several days to surface. First up was Xolile himself. An alert photographer snapped him leaving a night club at 5 in the morning with two blonde women. One of the girls earned a bit of money by kissing and telling the local newspaper two days later. "Xolile Dalindyebo is, like, huge, in every respect, you know what I mean?" she was quoted as saying. Allison despite herself was deeply hurt by it. She rebuked herself privately as being an old fool.

The other players teased him but it was only to Allison on Skype that he admitted he had paid the girl a grand to say it.

"Why?" asked Allison, surprised to find him doing something so nakedly egotistical.

"The Crusaders guys were calling me a poofdah in the scrums. I thought I needed to set the record straight. Plus after the game I was too knackered and drunk even to think about sex so I thought I might as well do the whole celebrity thing." he replied.

"Well you seem to have done that all right." Allison quite determinedly shrugged off her petty feelings of resentment.

The second incident involved the two centres, Lategan and Lewis. They found a bar and a fight still available around 4 in the morning. Unfortunately the fight was with three MMA fighters. MMA is the new best thing among martial arts fans - extreme fighters who fight no holds barred contests in cages.

Lategan sustained a season ending broken jaw while Lewis was hospitalised with a severe concussion for a few days. The Australian media went to town over this one - what titillated them the most was not the drunken brawling but the fact that the two Lions players had lost in a fight against considerably smaller men.

Xolile tweeted: *"We're professional rugby players who occasionally get into fights. Those guys are professional fighters who look for bigger drunk men in bars to show off..."*

Followers: 37, 345

With two make shift centres and the constant media attention, the game against the Auckland Blues was a disaster. The team was still recovering the titanic efforts against the Crusaders. Stupid aggression and two cards, one yellow and one red, put the seal on the Blues victory, by a surprisingly comfortable 20 points.

But the really rocking scandal was Andile's.

13

The meeting was a short one: Mike Chisholm and the five members of the "Tig" committee, including Xolile. That committee was the players' own internal police and disciplinary body. Andile was known to refer to them derisively as the 'Kapos'. Mike was businesslike and to the point.

"Andile was arrested this morning on a charge of statutory rape. After the Crusaders game he met a girl in a bar, had sex with her and left in the morning. The girl is only 17 and the family has photos of them having sex. We're sending him home as soon as he's released on bail. I wanted to tell you before the others…"

No one really knew what to say. Jan Cilliers prevaricated as best he could. "We can't say anything yet; we need to speak to the whole team."

Chisholm did his best to resist this notion but eventually agreed and the team congregated in the hotel board room within the hour.

Buoyed by numbers the team as a whole had plenty to say.

"This is a set up. Why would anyone take photos of their daughter having sex?"

"Where's Andile? Doesn't someone need to be with him in court? They run their courts here in a foreign language…"

"Yes, English." (laughter)

"It's the same scam that the Stormers had used against them two years ago. All they wanted was money then. We can buy them off."

"I saw that girl he went off with. She was damn nearly six foot tall, if she was 17 I am only 19..."

"And why's he being sent home? The case is not over."

Eventually Mike Chisholm held up his hand for silence. "The question is not whether she looked her age or not. Apparently her birth certificate says she is 17. While you're right that this is a scam, we got caught by it, Andile did anyway, and the team is going to suffer. I told you when we set off on tour to be careful with the locals but nobody listens to me. The bosses say they are not spending money to bail players out who fall foul of the law. They say it's our own problem. The bosses have hired a local law firm to protect Andile and the team's reputation only. They are in court with him as we speak. The lawyers say they'll get him bail and he can go home on promise to return when the case comes to court."

"How much money do they want?" asked Xolile.

"Don't know. They haven't given a figure but they talk about the stain on their family name and their need for recompense. Whatever they want, the franchise won't pay so the amount is not the issue."

"Yes it is. If it's not a huge amount we might be able to raise it or Andile might be able to get a loan and pay it back over time... the amount is everything."

"It's orders from the owners – Andile goes back to Joburg tonight and the court case takes its course."

Many players now joined in with complaints of the why who says and why should we listen to them variety.

Chisholm glared at Xolile but eventually had to agree as more and more of the team supported the position that it was too soon to send him back to Joburg. It was decided that Jan and Xolile would meet the family as soon as the lawyers could arrange it.

The meeting was held at a local hotel in a "breakaway room". The family, originally a clan of McGintys from Scotland, was in the process of emigrating from New Zealand to the Gold Coast in Australia. Xolile guessed that they had sunk their savings into a bar and grill that probably wasn't doing that well. The family seemed to have been suspicious that they were being lured into a rendezvous with the Lions that would end in bloodshed – they had brought a number of large young men with big jackets that hid firearms presumably. The girl, the plaintive, was not present.

The Lions were represented only by Jan, Xolile and a lawyer, Shahieda, from the local firm in the employ of the Lions. Shahieda's main interest seemed to be that neither Jan nor Xolile did anything to admit guilt or compromise some future huge court case that she and the firm were preparing to defend.

After introductions Dave McGinty, the father of the girl, assumed the spokesman role. He droned on for many minutes about the goodness of his daughter, how her name had been besmirched, how she might never recover. He produced a sheaf of supporting documents – her high school reports, photos of her in a school play, aptitude test for her chosen career of being an air hostess….

"She doesn't look 17," put in Jan. Her father duly placed a copy of her birth certificate on the table.

"How much recompense are you thinking of?" asked Xolile. He got a dirty look from their lawyer. Dave took a while before replying as if he were mentally calculating.

"Two hundred thousand, Aus dollars, I mean…." Jan and Xolile made a pantomime of astonishment, Jan even whistling in supposed surprise. "More or less," added Dave.

Xolile then spoke at some length. Jan noticed he rolled a little toy around his thumb and forefinger as he spoke. He emphasized how the team sought only to resolve this matter to everyone's satisfaction. He talked of Andile's background, how he came from a poor village in the Transkei, had numerous financial commitments to his family, how little he still earned after seven years of Super Rugby.

"Even if he agreed to this sum it would take him more than five years to pay it off and he probably doesn't have another five years in him as a professional rugby player. It simply can't work, it's impossible."

"Then we go to trial" put in one of the sons.

"Well, we do have access to some money in Australia that we could get to you within, say, ten days. It's in cash so no tax necessary - that will save you, I don't know, what is the tax rate here, forty percent?"

The lawyer made shh noises. Xolile ignored her.

"We could get you 15 thousand dollars within ten days." Jan looked at him in surprise now.

"That's way too little," said Dave, "we couldn't possibly settle on less than 120…"

It took them an hour to agree on thirty five thousand dollars to be delivered within ten days to Dave himself in Australia.

"Well, that went well" said Xolile as they left the hotel.

"Where are you going to get the money from?" Jan asked.

"Oh you know I worked in Australia for a year or so, saved some money without declaring it so it's just sitting with a friend doing nothing. We have to tell Andile where the money's coming from but please nobody else, particularly not Chisholm. We just say we have negotiated our way out of the trial, OK?"

Later that night on Skype to Allison, Xolile told her that he had realized that the easiest way to have everyone know something in the team was to swear someone to secrecy.

"South Africans are good at many things but keeping secrets is not one of them" he told her. "But I think I have a bigger problem: the coach has definitely taken against me. I'm still not sure how to handle him – he's got such an authoritarian attitude, it's insulting to the players…"

"Don't you need him to be on side with you if you want the next step?" said Allison. "And what is the next step?"

"I want to be captain" replied Xolile, and they both laughed companiably from thousands of kilometres away.

"Where did you get the all this money from in Australia?" she asked, "and how much more you do have?"

"It's a long story. I might tell you when I get back to Joburg – it's sort of 'in case' money held by a friend in cash, nothing in the bank. And there is quite a bit more – I was willing to go to 100,000 to get Andile off."

Xolile's fears were confirmed when he was left out of the starting fifteen and the reserves for the last game on tour against the

Hurricanes. He used the time to hop across the sea to get the money from his stock in Melbourne.

Andile said to him before he left: "I don't know how to repay you, this is like a get out of jail free card you've given me. I might even be able to hold on to my fiancé if the coverage is not too hard on me."

"It's no big deal, really," Xolile told him, "and as for repaying me, I might ask you to do something for me in the future…"

"Anything, anything, you know that…"

In the event, Andile and his fiancé parted ways acrimoniously as soon as he returned to Joburg. For the next six months or more the team was forced to hear stories of the big man's loneliness, or on his cruder days, his masturbatory marathons.

After all the ups and downs of the tour, the Lions managed to shrug off the two great victories they had had and be absolutely inept for the last game. They were slaughtered by 52 points to 12. The commentators referred to the critical absence of the "talismanic Dalindyebo" in the loss.

14

Back in Joburg with 9 points from their Australasian tour the Lions were finally out of contention for the playoffs. With two local matches, against the Cheetahs and the Bulls to finish their campaign for the year, attention in the camp was focused on recruitment and preparations for the next year.

Allison met Xolile in the Rosebank Hotel as soon as the shuttle dropped him in the City from the airport.

They had a brief moment of awkwardness as both almost embraced the other but then neither did, settling for a handshake.

"Good news, I think" she told him. She showed him an email from the management of Toulon rugby club in France. Rolling in money, they had offered Xolile a contract worth almost 3 million rand per year.

"I'm not really interested in this except as a bargaining counter" he told her. "Can we leak this offer to the newspapers?"

"Easily done," Allison told him, "but it is a lot of money. You're sure you're not interested?"

"You know now that I'm not short of money. Let's keep this as a last resort – I've still a long way to go with the Lions, I hope."

Xolile was restored to the Lions team for the last two matches. He scored three tries in the matches and the Lions lost against the Cheetahs but beat an off form Bulls team at Loftus Versveld. He was gratified to see that the notoriously one eyed fans in Pretoria were not hostile when he ran on the field, in fact he got a warm cheer. When he scored his predictably spectacular try from deep he was rewarded with prolonged applause and a brief chant of "Dagger".

15

Xolile came to lunch with Allison and the girls.

"You look bigger on TV," said Leah, her younger.

"That's 'cos I am bigger on TV" said Xolile.

"And how do you say your first name?" asked Leah.

"You click out the side of your mouth, like you might say giddyap to a horse, and then add olile... easy right?" They all practiced until they could do it reasonably fluently.

Allison and he moved on to the next steps as she served the lasagne.

"Will we still have this working arrangement if you're forced to go to France?" she asked him.

"Ja, forced to earn 4 million rand" put in Rosemary, the elder. The newspapers had reported the offer from Toulon the previous day, The Star leading with a front page report headed: "Dagger for France?" The price had gone up in the telling as well.

"Well let's see what happens tomorrow with the contract negotiations. The towel sponsorship is a plus, Allison. Please handle all the contract stuff and take 20% of the fee up front for yourself. At least you will have an income for a while."

Allison had pulled in a sponsorship from a local towel manufacturer. Xolile would be filmed scoring a try wearing only a bath sheet from the company.

"How much is 20% worth?" asked Rosemary, always the forward

one.

"Rose! It's rude to talk of money in such a crude way."

"About R200, 000 per year. Should keep you in air time and Jimmy Choos for a while." Xolile had no qualms about telling the kids how much their mother was earning.

16

The room was crowded when Xolile had his turn for the next year's contract negotiations. Chisholm and the other coaches were there, as well James Dlamini, the part owner who had made billions in computer supply to the government whose company had bought a controlling share in the Lions some two years previously. He had in tow a number of financial people and other corporate types, the introductions were too fast for Xolile to keep track of them.

"Dalindyebo, I understand from the newspapers you are headed to France." Mike Chisholm fired the opening salvo.

"Not necessarily. I'd like to stay with the Lions for next year, if you'll have me."

Dlamini cut in. "You have to realize that we can't pay you anything like what they are offering you overseas, we simply don't have that sort of cash around. You're, what, on a 400K package now, right? That's a vast increase, way beyond our means."

"I'll stay for, say, a 30% salary increase… and I want to be captain." Xolile delivered this in a matter of fact tone.

Mike Chisholm was instantly furious and showed it. He banged his fist on the table making the finance people jump.

"What rubbish! Who gives you the right to lay down preconditions? It's the coach who decides the captain not some johnny come lately with a big ego and a bigger social media personality…"

"Hang on, hang on, Mike. Dalindyebo, why do you want to be captain? Mike is right that you have very little experience at this level.

Is it just about the title or do you feel you can bring something more to the team?" James Dlamini had a reputation as a dynamic business man, a comer in the corporate world.

"I believe I have a lot to offer. I want to be captain because I want to play a role in bringing new ideas and techniques to the team. I believe the fans have been loyal too long – the Lions have never even been in the play offs since the expanded Super Rugby league began ten years ago. Mike is a good coach but he's too set in his ways, too school masterish, he doesn't think much of the intelligence of the players on the field..."

Dlamini cut off Chisholm's next response. "Wait" he said, "Mike, I think we need to discuss this in private. Dalindyebo, won't you wait outside the room for say half an hour, get some coffee we'll call you back shortly.

Xolile left and Chisholm gave full vent to his spleen. "This peacock thinks he's too good for the rest of us. He's constantly undermining my authority, challenging me at every turn. I have a contract - you can't make him captain above my wishes, I'll go to court and take you for every sent you have..."

"No threats please, Mike. This is a friendly discussion. You must appreciate my position: I'm a fan, sure, but this is an investment, our company's stake in the Lions. I need to show returns for my shareholders. What the Dagger says is correct – we've waited a hell of a long time for the Joburg team to match the ambitions of its fans. This guy has over 50,000 followers on twitter – I know because I'm one of them – last week in a nothing game against the Cheetahs there were almost 35,000 people in the crowd at Ellis Park. And it seemed to me that about a quarter of them were black. This is our dream - that the Lions become a successful team that is supported by black and white fans. We're getting this guy to play for us at a 60% discount compared to what a glamour side is prepared to pay for him in Europe. What would you do in my position?"

Mike Chisholm realized the tide was swinging away from him. "All very well but does he have the support of the team? I know some of the players think just like me – that he's a flash kid with some talent whose interests are only about himself."

"We'll have to ask the team," said Dlamini with finality.

That night Xolile phoned Andile. "You know that favour I did you? Well the payback is coming more quickly than I anticipated."

"Whatever you need, I'll do" promised Andile.

Allison met Xolile at his favourite coffee bar in Parktown.

"Things are moving swiftly now; I want you to put an insert in maybe The Star's website breathing rumours of a player revolt in the Lions…"

"Will do. How specific do you want it?"

"I'll leave that to you…. But mainly I want a report of player unhappiness, I think that's the main element."

17

The Star website, June 30th: *Rumours are swirling around the Lions camp of unhappiness with the management style of Coach Mike Chisholm. According to unconfirmed reports the issue that has brought matters to a head is the appointment of Xolile 'Dagger' Dalindyebo to the position of captain for the 2015 season. A number of meetings have been held to address this crisis but no resolution is in sight.*

The next morning Andile handed into the bosses a letter signed by all the current players calling for Xolile to be made captain.

The Star, July 14th:

In a major shakeup in order to pursue glory in the coming year the The Lions announced several changes to their management.

Cup winning New Zealand coach Mike Chisholm is now Gauteng Director of Rugby and will take charge of all Gauteng teams from under 19's to seniors. Lions CEO James Dlamini said yesterday that the management team believes that Chisholm's influence would be felt for many years as he instils modern methods and disciplines into the younger teams.

Xolile "Dagger" Dalindyebo was named captain for the year of the super rugby team which will now be coached by Willem Pretorius, coach of the provincial side since 2010. Andile Phike, former Springbok hooker will be vice captain.

Fans were reported to be delighted that the reported move of The Dagger to France is no longer an option.

Xolile met with James Dlamini in his office the next day.

"Satisfied?" asked Dlamini. "You can work with Willem?"

"Very, he was my coach when I first came back to Joburg. But if we're to be championship material we need new players... I need a budget to buy some special individuals." Xolile wasn't sure how far this new relationship with the boss would go.

"Well we've lost four contracted players to retirement and overseas, so you can use those contracts as a start. How many special individuals do you think we need?"

"I think around seven. The strength in the team is the conveyor belt of really great hard working loose forwards – we can use all six in the team and as replacements. We need to replace Jan and we need much more quality reserves in the front row, more talent at half back and we need a finisher – about seven players."

"A finisher? Isn't that your job?"

"You know Jona Lomu never scored a try against South Africa – if you mark a player with enough people you can neutralize him. But Christian Cullen in the same team averaged more than a try a match against South Africa. We blocked the space around Lomu and Cullen ran in the tries."

"So you reckon while teams are marking you the new finisher will score the tries?"

"Exactly."

"Well you had better get recruiting then. Four contracts first and come to me for after that."

Xolile, Allison, Andile and Jan met for dinner later that day. Andile had brought his cousin, Noluthando, for Xolile to look over. She was an aspirant model and gloriously beautiful.

Allison felt a simmering resentment as she took in her glowing skin and immaculate make up. Beautiful and young, she thought, how unfair was that?. Xolile was courteous to her but seemed uninterested in her as a partner, she was pleased to note.

The five of them raised their glasses as the first of the wine was poured.

"To the Magnificent Seven" said Andile and they all repeated it and drank the overpriced wine…

The Magnificent Seven (1960) is an American western film directed by John Sturges and starring Yul Brynner, Eli Wallach and Steve McQueen. The picture is an Old West-style remake of Akira Kurosawa's Japanese-language film *Seven Samurai* (1954). The supporting cast features Charles Bronson, Robert Vaughn, James Coburn, Brad Dexter, and Horst Buchholz. They play a group of seven American gunfighters hired to protect a small agricultural village in Mexico from a group of marauding native bandits led by Calvera (Eli Wallach). The film's musical score was composed by Elmer Bernstein. In 2013, the film was selected for preservation in the United States National Film Registry by the Library of Congress as being "culturally, historically, or aesthetically significant".

Wikipedia 2015

PART TWO

18

If Xolile thought that finding new magnificent talent was going to be easy, the next few weeks disabused him of that notion.

"The scouts are everywhere, signing up kids from townships, private schools, junior leagues, you name it," he told Allison. "You know I went to an under 11 tournament in Mogale last week – there were scouts there looking over kids who were only 10 years old. It's going to be tough finding talent that no one else has... I need your help, I don't know which way to turn."

"I'm trying all I can" she replied. "I've been in contact with a guy called Pote Fourie in Welkom. He says he might have one or two individuals for you but he was cagy. Eventually he came out with the question of money – if he finds you players he wants to be paid for it."

"I know of him, he's been a tigerish flank for the Welkom team for the last decade. Tell him if we take any of his introductions he'll get paid the agent's fee – I think it's 5% of the contract."

Allison made a brief note in her diary and then pulled out an internet printout from within her briefcase.

"And then there's this. I don't know if you're interested in this guy.... He sent you a comment on the Youtube video of your try – and he's holidaying in Cape Town as we speak."

The report stated that Jeremy Gandolfini, former England and

Canberra Brumbies flyhalf was holidaying in Cape Town, staying with friend Tony Syngin-Johnson at his Fraanschoek holiday home.

"What did he say about the try?" asked Xolile.

"Here he wrote: *great try – check out mine against Saracens for a better one*. And then he sent you a link to his try, just let me get it up on the laptop…."

They watched in silence as the two minute clip of, surely, thought Xolile, one of the really great individual tries of all time. Gandolfini displayed dazzling footwork, a hand off like a jab from Mohammed Ali, great acceleration, a final flourish at the touchline as he beat what seemed to be the whole of the Saracens team.

"Bad missed tackle there – at the end just before he goes into the 22. But it still is a great try. Tell him I want him to do exactly the same for the Lions next Saturday."

"But the Lions are not playing till next season."

"Let's see if he knows that." Xolile was silent for a moment. "He's a great talent – but he's trouble, discipline, bad attitude to authority…. Do we need his kind of problem in the team?"

"But he played for England – isn't he an exceptional player at his best?"

"He certainly is… OK let's go see him in Cape Town. Can you get away for a day?"

19

On the plane to Cape Town they poured over the internet printouts of Gandolfini. Xolile was surprised, and pleased, to learn that he was, in fact, black by South African standards. His father was West Indian, mother a determined English lass who had sent him to the best schools.

He was identified early as a potential match winner at fly half for England, the newspapers called him the new Jonny Wilkinson. He played a handful of games for England in 2010 but then poor form and the inevitable disagreements with the coaches saw him discarded.

He spent a season playing for a Super team in Australia where the same pattern emerged – initially a tremendous boost to the local club but later discipline and so so performances soured his stay. His contract was not renewed at the end of the season. The previous season he had played for the Sale Sharks in England where he failed to shine in a poor team.

"Didn't he date the queen for a while as well?"

Allison laughed. "Distant relative but he hangs with the rich and famous – that was one of the criticisms of him in Australia."

They hired a car from Cape Town airport and drove the hour to the rich and picturesque little town of Fraanschoek. They had decided on the plane to cold call on him, no phone calls before. Xolile said he wanted to see what kind of shape he was in before they made an offer.

"Do you know," said Allison, apropos nothing at all, "that in the new South African version of Monopoly the most expensive property to own is Franschoek? Do you know the game? In the English version the most expensive cards are Park Lane and Mayfair."

Without children to entertain on rainy afternoons Xolile had no idea what she was talking about.

They found the Syngin-Johnson's estate without difficulty. It was a small holding, really, rather than an out and out farm, with some vineyards and a simple but sumptuous white bricked building ended the curved driveway through the grape lands. Maddeningly, Jeremy Gandolfini was not there. The butler told them that he was probably brunching at a local eatery. They made their way back into the little town and found him at, of all things, a Sushi and Cocktail Bar.

They could see Gandolfini and a bunch of other people in the distance but the restaurant was full, waiting time about an hour, they were told. Allison watched him intently. He was a dramatically good looking man, dark and brooding, was how she would have described him. He had his arm around several of the girls at the table.

 Standing at the entrance Xolile caught the eye of the sushi chef and greeted him tentatively in Japanese. He later told Allison that across the world the Chinese now dominated sushi chef positions and only the fanciest employed a genuine Japanese sushi chef. In this event not only was the chef Japanese but he was delighted to speak his language for the first time in a number of weeks. They found themselves whisked to a table not very far from Gandolfini's group.

They settled themselves down and ordered drinks. Gandolfini was part of a group of nine, five men and four women. Their table was littered with sushi and drink debris.

Xolile was just about to brace him when Gandolfini noticed him.

"Hey man! Aren't you The Dagger?" he shouted across at him.

Xolile got up and shook hands with him. "This guy," said Gandolfini to the others, "is one of the world's great rugby players, no really" he emphasized when the group looked sceptical.

Allison and Xolile joined their table while introductions were done and drinks ordered.

"Have you come to offer me a job?" asked Gandolfini mischievously.

"We've flown from Joburg to see you, yes" allowed Xolile, "what are you doing at the moment?"

"I think I'm what you might call between engagements ..." General merriment followed from the table. "So I'd like to play for the Lions next season if you'll have me."

"We need to speak privately, perhaps" said Xolile.

"Nah, these are my best friends in the world," said Gandolfini, "you can say anything in front of them."

Xolile gave a shrug, as though it was no real matter to him. "The Lions are looking for a top flyhalf for 2015, it's true. But we want a team man, someone with a strong commitment to the good of the team – and the team would be strongly committed to that individual. We are looking for someone who can take our attacking options to new level. But we don't want an individualist pursuing personal glory." Xolile delivered this as though it were a prepared speech.

Various people at the table spoke then, chief amongst them Tony Syngin-Johnson.

"Jeremy is simply the best there is – he's a rugby genius."

"That may be so but we aim to win the Super Rugby competition by playing the most progressive adventurous rugby. The more we succeed the greater the pressures on top players. We need someone with flair who takes orders. Are you that sort of person?"

"Damned right I am," replied Gandolfini, "discipline is my middle name. Here, let me pour you some of our excellent Chardonnay." He rose to go around to other side of the overflowing table. As he picked up the bottle to return to Xolile and Allison's side of the table he stumbled slightly.

"Whoops" he said and suddenly giggled. Allison glanced at Xolile. They both realized he was quite drunk at 11 30 in the morning. As usual Xolile was inscrutable but she fancied she could read a contemptuous look on his face, or maybe she was projecting her own contempt, she thought to herself.

"In this project the past counts nothing, your reputation – zero. All that matters to us is what you can and will do for the team." Xolile's voice was soft now, almost a regretful tone, it seemed to Allison. "Have you still got that drive, that commitment that marked you out in the first years of your career?"

"Spare me this management double speak bullshit. I do what I do and I do it well, like the Dylan song. If I play for the Lions they'll be glad to have hired me."

"You've not convinced me of that at all. Perhaps you should come up to Joburg and speak to Willem, the coach."

"What do you mean you're unconvinced? What do you know of me anyway?"

"I know you've had quite a bit to drink before lunch on Wednesday morning – if you were me would this inspire confidence?"

"Well, fuck you" said Gandolfini, "who asked you to disturb our brunch with insults and aggression? You can fuck off back to Johannesburg and take your silent body guard with you..."

"Fair enough" said Xolile, "sorry everybody for the interruption. But what your friend said about you is true – you are potentially one of the world's great players. Let us make you a star again, rather than waste your talent like this. " He rose to leave and then, almost as afterthought, handed Jeremy Gandolfini a piece of paper with his phone number on. "In case you change your mind..."

They headed back to the airport. "What a wasted trip, I'm sorry" she told Xolile.

"Not at all" he replied, "I expect to hear from him soon."

On the plane back Allison found a whole series of Utube clips of Gandolfini in various stages of his career.

Xolile shook his head sadly. "A rare talent," he told Allison.

20

The next trip planned was to meet Pote Fourie in Welkom. Allison cried off: "I don't like just being a spectator like I was in Cape Town."

So Xolile went alone to Welkom by car. Pote had told him he would be in the Railway Hotel after 5 pm. The hotel was a lovely old example of Victorian architecture, with a large balcony running the length of the first floor.

Pote sat with a bunch of his rugby and work mates inside the 'Ladies Bar'. There were in fact no ladies there but the room was familiar to Xolile because he had been in a hundred like it. Although smoking was no longer allowed in the bar, years of cigarettes had permeated the furnishings and the curtains so that it smelt as though someone has just finished a pack over your shoulder.

The predictable black and white photographs of the early years of the gold mining industry in Welkom completed the look of faded glory.

"Ah the Dagger has punctured our space!" shouted Pote in greeting as Xolile entered. Introductions were extended as each member of his entourage got up to shake his hand.

"Great try against the Crusaders," said one man in his sixties with a nicotine stained handle bar moustache. Pote said he would show Xolile both players the next morning.

"But tonight we drink!" he bellowed.

At 10 pm Xolile was onto his fourth beer and feeling a bit tiddly. He was deep in conversation with moustache, he was told his name but had forgotten it, who was, Xolile discovered in that drunken state of bonhomie he had entered, a man of exceptional intelligence.

"You know that thing that all New Zealand teams like to do?" said Moustache.

"Yeah, win..." replied Xolile. Both of them thought that was very funny.

"No, not that one. You know how they plan to score in the ten minutes before and after half time? They suddenly up their intensity and the whole team plays like they are possessed. Then they score and they slow it right down for the next few minutes to recover, right?"

"Right."

"Well how would it be if instead of doing it only around half time, the captain calls, I don't know, top speed or something and the players try and up the tempo, harass their opponents, throw in quickly, get the game going as fast as possible maybe at surprising times, say half way through the half or just after someone has been sent off. Then at another signal, the team slows it right down, walks to the lineouts as though they are going through mud, take forever to hear the line out calls, the ball falls over when they kick a penalty, argue with the ref – in short do everything to disrupt the other team's rhythm."

Xolile looked at moustache over his beer glass. Yes, he thought to himself, this is what is beautiful about this country: here's a bar in the middle of nowhere and a man who is a fan tells you of a theory and suddenly you are thinking he's absolutely right...

"We'll try it in the coming season – and we'll call it the 'moustache' move," he told him.

21

That morning Xolile was feeling at his worst as he bounced along with Pote in his old Cortina towards the Free Gold hostel. Pote, by contrast, was ebullient and showed little effect of the binge they had had the night before.

"There are two guys I want to show you" he told me, "the first one works in the canteen here at the mine."

They walked through long corridors before emerging at into a giant hall with stainless steel tables. Xolile followed Pote through a set of swing doors.

"Hey, Tsego," he shouted at a figure in an apron, "meet The Dagger."

The figure in the apron turned and the words 'sumo wrestler' popped into Xolile's mind. The man was a giant – he must have been just short of two metres tall and easily weighed 150 kilograms. Pote's eyes sparkled naughtily as he said to Xolile: "Tsego plays prop – he's pretty good."

Xolile shook hands with Tsego – his were huge and warm and slightly damp. He was an enormously shy man and as he chatted to Xolile about his history – he had grown up in a small dry town in Mpumalanga called Ogies – it was sometimes difficult to hear what he was saying. Xolile promised to phone him from Joburg and arrange a trial and a fitness assessment.

As they walked on he said to Pote: "Can that guy actually run? Is he one of those fat boys whose thighs rub together?"

"He's faster than you" said Pote laconically.

"Really?"

"Let's just say that if that I put a plate of food on that side of the field I know who would get to it first…" Pote chortled to himself delightedly.

They walked on. Sometime last night Pote had let Xolile know that he worked for the mine – but not as a sports officer. He was an underground miner and perversely proud of it.

"I do the second-shittiest job in the world," he said.

"Who then does the shittiest?" Xolile asked

"The guys who work under me," his eyes were twinkling again.

Pote seemed to be popular with workers – several said hello to him and got a grunt in reply, while one even got an effusive greeting in Fanagalo and a punch on the shoulder.

"Tell me about this man we're going to see."

"Jim Mahlangu? Three years ago suddenly the papers are full of this Matric kid in Soweto who's running the hundred metres in just on ten seconds. He gets a scholarship to the mine here, and a reasonable salary, all he has to do is train and run races in the mine colours. Some people said in three years, like now, he could beat Usain Bolt."

"I've never heard of him," Xolile admitted. "What's he done since?"

"A boarding school of women, a swimming pool of beer, a sack of dagga. He won't train, often won't run in races. He's been trying to change jobs, even go to another mine. Half the bosses want to persuade him to run, the other half want to boot him out."

"Does he play rugby?"

"No idea. All I know for sure is that he can still run bloody fast."

There were four men sitting around a packing case in the centre of the dormitory. Pote strode over as though he owned the place. The four men looked at them with only scant interest. Quart bottles of beer stood on the case and at their feet. It was obvious that they'd been sitting in the same position for hours.

"Jim!" said Pote. A stocky, powerfully built young man got slowly to his feet. As he rose, Xolile had a glimpse of a very well defined thigh.

"This is Xolile Dalindyebo," said Pote with a wave in his direction.

"Hi," Xolile said, "I'm here to make you famous again." With that, from about two metres away, he lobbed the rugby ball he was holding in his right hand at Jim.

Jim grabbed at the ball with both hands. It bounced off his fingertips, knocked a beer bottle off the crate and skittered away under the iron bedstead nearby.

22

That same afternoon, Pote, Jim and Xolile went to a school rugby field to attempt to teach Jim the rudiments of the game.

"Rugby is a simple game, really," Pote told him. "The aim is to put the ball down, with your hands, behind the goalpost. The opposing team tries to do the same behind yours. To do that one can only move the ball forward in two ways – you carry it forward or you kick it forward, *yabona*?"

Jim gave him an indulgent half-smile. He seemed to regard them as the average person might respond to a couple of friendly aliens who asked him to view their spacecraft – not quite know whether to laugh or wonder at.

"Your job will be only one – when you get the ball you go for the corner flag – that one there or the other side if you're on that side of the field. If you're tackled you roll over with the tackler with your back to the goal line, count to three and then release the ball. One of the loose forwards will come and pick it up – hopefully," Xolile told him.

"Or even more hopefully you don't get tackled at all." Pote tossed the ball to Jim. He dropped it. "You're too tense, man. You've got to make your hand soft, soft as a woman's doos."

Xolile marveled anew at Pote's gift for crudity.

"Here. Try again." Pote lobbed the ball at Jim from a distance of about five metres. Jim bounced it off his fingertips, bounced it on the ground once in front of him, juggled it awhile and then clasped it to his chest at a half stagger.

"How's that?" he asked with a shy grin.

"It's shit, that's what it is." Pote clearly had no ideas about indulging Jim during his first touches of a rugby ball. "It's called a knock-on – you can only carry the ball forward or kick it forward, remember? Get it? Chuck it here."

They watched as the ball sailed over their heads. One of a small crowd of schoolboys who had gathered to gawp fetched the ball. "Hello Pote", "Hoe gaan dit, Pote?" they said respectfully. There was no doubt as to which of the three of them was best known – on this rugby field at least.

Xolile showed Jim how to hand off an opponent – the equivalent of the jab in boxing but delivered with the open hand while running at speed. Jim had boxed a bit "when he was young", he told them and he took to it easy and naturally. After a while they gave up trying to pass the ball to him but had a little training tableau – on the twenty two metre line Xolile would spin around and hand the ball to Jim who would tuck it under his arm and run for the corner flag with Pote attempting to cut him off. "Run" is not actually the word for what Jim did though – he flowed along the touchline at a speed that was breathtaking. Xolile had never seen a human being run that fast with a rugby ball. The first two times they tried this set piece, Jim went around Pote easily – Pote then set himself almost directly in line with the corner flag and knocked Jim down with a tackle of crunching brutality.

"No," said Pote, "that shouldn't have happened. I was coming in much too upright. You tried to hand me off on the chest – no good. If the tackler comes in straight up you hit him in the face, the forehead, the throat. Get it? Now this time I'm going to come in too low. You hit me here, on the top of the shoulder, then when I go down you step out of the tackle. Got it?"

Jim did and got away the next time. From then on Pote came in at what he called "pens high", or what the rest of the world called the epigastrium. A real contest developed between the two of them. Jim instinctively dropped towards the touchline to give himself more space while Pote came in as hard and determined as the really great loose forward that he had been. It was no surprise to Xolile that Pote won hands down – in the next nine pieces Jim got through only twice.

They had a rest for a while. Jim and Pote were panting. Pote lit a cigarette and after a while Jim took one too. He blew a smoke ring out. "I've got two questions," he said suddenly. Xolile realised that this was the first unsolicited comment he'd heard him make. Pote and Xolile sat up straighter. "Where's the point of my running for the corner flag in a match if almost every time someone like Pote stops me?"

It was such a good question from someone who didn't know the first thing about rugby that Xolile moved over to hug him. At the last moment he clapped him on the shoulder instead.

"Not a bad question. But in fact, in total, you got past Pote five times out of fourteen; that's good. Pote's probably a better tackler than any wing in the country at the moment. If you were running against provincial wings you would have beaten two, three, maybe even four more; that's a good percentage. In a game, a good game for us, you might get the ball in a one on one situation maybe three times – that's a try for you every time we play well."

"And tackling?" asked Pote. "At the highest level every player has to tackle well."

Xolile shrugged with an offhandedness that he wasn't entirely sure was justified. "Tackling isn't an art, it's a skill. Our defensive coach will teach him to tackle in a few weeks or so."

Jim had more to contribute: "But what about kicking the ball then instead of running into this other guy – the wing, or is he a fullback? Or why not run on the inside of him towards the other goal post?" Jim was really cooking with good ideas now – as Pote had said, rugby was a simple game.

"No. Let's be clear about this. Your job is to get the ball and go as hard as you can for the corner flag. When you've played for, say, three months, we'll teach you other things; for now concentrate on what you can do. In this situation, the one we've been practicing, you're already Currie Cup, maybe even Super Rugby, standard. Don't try and do anything else."

"What about passing? And tackling? Or coming up through the middle between the centres?" asked Pote. Pote flicked his cigarette on to a pile of dry grass. Xolile looked at him in irritation. "We're teaching him to score, sometimes, spectacular tries. Get it?" Pote nodded.

"I've another question." Jim's face was impassive. "Why is it that Pote and I get out of breath, and bruised, and you just give me the ball and do nothing else? Don't you ever run or tackle?"

Pote's face crinkled as he lay back in the sun. He waved an indolent arm at Xolile; so answer, it seemed to say.

Half a dozen responses flitted through Xolile's brain: I am too small; tackling isn't my job, it is Pote's; I am the trainer here; I have just landed a well paid job and can't afford to be injured at the beginning of the season …

"It's because," he said, getting to his feet to signal a return to practice, "I'm the baas."

23

Xolile and Willem Pretorius sat in the juice bar of the gym two weeks later. In the distance they could see Jim Mahlangu lifting weights with dogged determination.

"This kid you found is terrific, in some respects, anyway. For someone who's never played before he's a natural. His passing is improving every day and he takes the pass well too now..."

"Great," said Xolile, "let's get him a couple of games with the provincial team and see if he's ready for the big show next season."

"But that Tsego," Willem shook his head. "He can scrum but he's a butterball – can't tackle, very unfit, no real feel for the game. We could keep him on as a practice mate for the real team but I can't see him being Super Rugby standard."

"We thought as much when we met him in Welkom," replied Xolile. "It's your call – could he be a good prop, say, in two years, if we keep him and train him?"

"Maybe – let's contract him for the provincial team for 6 months and see... There's something I didn't tell you, maybe should have a while ago."

"Yeah, what?"

"A guy came and saw me when I was provincial coach about a year ago. He was straight off the train from Zimbabwe. He said he played front row but to me he looked more like a loose forward, smallish man, weighed only 80 kilograms. I told him straight that he wasn't the physical type we were looking for. I referred him to a club and he's been playing for Pirates for the past year..."

"And?"

"Rudi, the coach of Pirates, an old friend from Monument school days, tells me he's become something special. I think we should look at him – Pirates play the University of Johannesburg on Saturday afternoon."

"OK, pick me up from home at 3 on Saturday. Now who else do we have with potential from the under 20's?"

24

Xolile sat with Willie at the Pirates club. It was a freezing cold winter's afternoon with that dry Highveld cold that crept into one's bones. The object of their attention was a Zimbabwean born prop with the name of Chimurenga Tongona. He was from a middle class family in Harari and had attended Churchill School, a colonial relic based on the British public schools.

"Not exactly a huge presence in the loose, is he?" said Xolile.

"No, but he gets around; wait until scrum time," Willem answered.

Five minutes later the first scrum of the game came around. Both Xolile and Willem exclaimed in unison as Tongona in the tight head position in effect cut his opposing loose head in half. The scrum ended in a penalty for Pirates.

"Impressive," said Xolile, "is he doing it legally or has he got some kind of funny technique that gives him such an advantage?"

"I can't be completely sure but from here it looks like he's doing it with pure strength. I'll put the glasses on him at the next scrum."

They met him at a coffee bar in Melville after the game. Xolile looked him up and down after they had shaken hands.

"Jesus, Willie, this guy is barely any bigger than me. How much do you weigh, Chimurenga?"

"Please call me Chimmy," he said, "and I weigh 85 kilograms, up from 81 six months ago." His voice was cultured. Xolile thought if he closed his eyes he would never have guessed he was speaking to a black man.

"That's very small for a top flight tight head" put in Willem.

"Look" said Chimmy, "I know who you guys are and if you are recruiting for the Super 15 side, of course I'm interested. But, how can I say this without sounding arrogant? I'm a born again person and I don't take kindly, Dagger, to your use of the Lord's name in vain. I hope you're not offended by my saying this…"

"I'll bear that in mind in the future," replied Xolile drily. "Willie we've got six months until the new season. Could you build his weight up to, say 105, by then?"

"Hard to say. I would have to get an opinion from the fitness coaches, but, yes, I think it can be done. Maybe if we put him on something special…?"

"I don't want to hear the details really. But if you think it can be done that's good enough for me" said Xolile and held out his hand again to Chimmy. "Welcome to the Lions and the Magnificent Seven…"

25

The Up and Under by Allison Meyer

The tactic of the ball kicked high in the air by the team in possession, with the aim of recovering possession if the defending team drops or fails to control the ball, is a common one.

The tactic has been around for decades, initially called the Gary Owen after one of the first clubs to use the kick in Wales. Nowadays the kick is often called a 'bomb' because it falls to earth and, unless it is well controlled by the defending team, can cause a great deal of damage.

All codes of rugby have the up 'n under as a potential tactic.

In Rugby League a rule change reduced the use of the bomb – now if the ball is caught on the full in the in goal area, a 20 metre tap restart results for the defending team.

It is probably used mostly in Union these days. Union kickers, usually flyhalves, but maybe scrumhalves too, practice for hours to get the ball, firstly, high enough, and, secondly, to bring it down precisely a metre or two outside the opponents twenty two.

Thus we have the ideal special characteristics of the perfect bomb – it must be high enough, and hence in the air for long enough, to enable the attacking team to run on to the contact area; ideally the ball should spin end over end in the air to make catching it cleanly as difficult as possible; and finally it should be as close to the tryline as possible but not over the twenty two metre line. The tactic of kicking in the air is limited by the safety of the twenty two metre area where the ball may be marked and no further charging of the player permitted until the defender has kicked the ball again.

In 2007 South Africa won the world cup with an absolute dedication to the up and under, labelled now the kick-chase game. The kick was allied to two very fast kamikaze style wings who would bring the jumper down and sometimes spoil the presentation of the ball sufficiently so that their own loose forwards could win the ball back.

The criticisms of the up and under were loud and sustained, particularly in Australasia, but, because the current rules favour the tactic somewhat, many top teams regard it as the most potent weapon in their armoury. As we speak we could say the rugby union world is divided between those teams that use it and those that spurn it in favour of keeping the ball in hand. Several New Zealand provincial teams do not use the up 'n under at all; but the national side in New Zealand, particularly in big games, use the up 'n under when they are tied down in their own half.

If we now follow the links below to the two clips on our website we can see two common scenarios from a kick chase. In the first one, the kick is poor, the Lions fullback takes the ball well and initiates a counter attack. In this case, a try results a few minutes later as a result of the space found from the back after the kick. In the second clip, the fullback takes the ball well but is not sufficiently protected by his forwards. The Lions' opponents, in this case the Cheetahs, swarm over the fullback on the ground, he fails to release for fear a try will result and the Cheetahs get a kickable penalty.

26

Willie, Xolile and Andile, newly named as vice-captain for the coming Super 15 season, sat in the stand of the grounds of the Pumas rugby team in Nelspruit. The stadium had been built for the 2010 Soccer World Cup and was one of the unusual purpose built grounds - in that it was used occasionally by the Pumas provincial side. Almost all the soccer world cup stadia weren't used at all. The stadium was a spectacular boat motif design seating maximally 45,000 people. Today if there were 2,000 spectators it was a lot.

They were watching the Pumas demolishing the Boland side. Their focus was on the Pumas half back pairing, namely scrumhalf Jason Schwartz and flyhalf Van Wyk de Vries. Opinions amongst the three talent scouts were heavily divided. Andile thought the de Vries the flyhalf was pretty good – a big man who defended his channel very effectively. Willie and Xolile thought he was nothing special – South African flyhalfs were traditionally large and good defenders.

"Surely we're looking for more than that," said Xolile, "we want a flyhalf who can create opportunities to score and to dictate the game, know when to defend and when to attack. I see none of that from this guy."

Andile was not convinced. "At the moment we've got nothing in the flyhalf stakes, isn't he better than nothing?"

"It's early days yet" said Xolile with a faith he didn't really feel.

The question of the scrumhalf, a stocky coloured kid with quick hands and a bad kicking game, was also disputed. Here Andile and Willie were united in the belief that he was nothing out of the ordinary while Xolile thought he had a lot of potential.

"What exactly do you see in this kid?" asked Andile.

"Well" began Xolile but as he paused momentarily Schwartz kicked the ball ahead from the Boland 10 metre line straight into touch. They could hear the groans from the Pumas forward pack from the stands. Willie and Andile seemed to find this very amusing and chortled away to each other for a minute or two, flinging sideways glances at Xolile. He, too, after a while was carried away by their mood and, almost grudgingly, began to chuckle.

"Forget the kicking nonsense," he said, "we wouldn't want our scrumhalf to kick much anyway so we would tell him to cut it out. And if we do want him to play a kicking role than we can train him to do it properly. It seems to me, Willie, that anyone can be taught to do box kicks, kicks in field just behind the opposing forwards.... No I want you to look at what he does have – a pretty good pass, good coaching could probably make it better, and, most of all, attitude. When the ball is presented at the end of a ruck or maul he wants it, he's focused only on that ball and getting it to his back line quickly. That's the main attribute of a good scrumhalf."

The others were largely unconvinced until ten minutes before the end. The Pumas were solidly on the attack and a series of 'pick and go's had led them to within five metres of the Boland line. The Boland forwards resisted manfully and all sixteen players from both sides hurled themselves at each other. Suddenly the ball was visible but buried by the legs of several Puma players. Schwartz bellowed at them to move, swooped on the ball and flung a perfect pass out to the inside centre, all in one movement. All three Lions representatives in the stand rose to their feet and applauded. The crowd was small enough for their praise to be noticed by everyone, even some of the players.

"Now I see it" said Andile, "that was almost as good as Aaron Smith for New Zealand."

"Ok" echoed Willie, "Ok…"

They met him after the game. Jason Schwartz was in person not that impressive a physique. He was a short, almost tubby man and he had a bad squint.

After introductions were done he asked if he could speak in Afrikaans.

"Certainly" said Xolile and handed over to Willie. He tuned out briefly and thought of flyhalfs. New Zealand seemed to have hundreds of flyhalfs, couldn't we buy one of those, he wondered to himself.

When his concentration returned to the conversation before him it seemed to have turned to a different topic entirely. It seemed for some reason that they were talking about hiring his brother!

"Willie?" he said enquiringly.

"Oh ja, Dagger, let me bring you up to speed…" Willie looked a little uncomfortable, "It seems that Jason lives with his brother and for him to come to Joburg we would have to find a place for the brother on the team."

"And who's his brother, does he at least play rugby?" asked Xolile, his irritation becoming visible.

"Oh yes" put in Jason with a thick Northern Cape accent, "he played flank this afternoon with me. It's Chris, my older brother. He looks after me, always has done."

He motioned for a man lurking in the background. "This is my brother, Chris" he said to Xolile with a degree of pride.

Xolile shook hands with Chris with his heart sinking. While the brother was better looking than Jason he was hardly any bigger.

Chris took over and was clearly used to speaking for Jason. "The thing is this" he began, "our parents died when we were young – I was 16 and Jason was only 9. I swore to them that I would look after him and I have done ever since, got him through school, not easy to do in Taung I can tell you. And then we moved to Nelspruit and the Pumas two years ago. We love it here and if Jason gets an opportunity to play in the big show, I'll be happy – but I must go with him."

Xolile put his head in his hands briefly in a rare show of frustration. "Chris, you're obviously a good player" he lied, having not noticed him once in the game they had just finished watching, "but you've got to realize that we think that Jason is a rare talent – a natural quick scrummie that we hope to grow into a very fine player over the next couple of years. In this country we don't have many good scrumhalves – but good flanks, we're awash with them. I'll tell you straight now that you have no chance of making the Super Rugby squad, there at least six loose forwards ahead of you…"

"I think you don't understand. When my mother died I swore to her on her dying bed that I would take care of Jason. It's not easy when you come from a poor community where the easy options – alcohol, drugs, crime, you name it – cripple young people. If Jason is going to be a star that would be great but my job is not done yet. I won't let him live in a place where I am not and that's that."

Xolile looked at Willie who shook his head eloquently. "I can't keep calling in favours from the provincial side. They have their own competition to win, their own team to build," said Willie.

"Look" said Andile, "by the end of the year Jason will be twenty two, right?" They both nodded a reply. "Well how about we find a place for both of you to live till the end of the year. If all goes well Jason will be first choice for the Lions Super Rugby team and Chris will try and get a contract with the provincial side."

"And if he doesn't?" asked Willie.

"Then Chris goes back to the Pumas and leaves us to make sure that Jason stays on the straight and narrow."

"No" replied Chris firmly, "we're a, what you call it, a package deal. It's both of us or neither of us..."

They argued it back and forth for a while and then by agreement they would wait to hear if the bosses would agree to a special contract for Chris. The Lions then started the three hour drive back to Joburg.

27

Sunday and Xolile was lunching with Allison and the girls again.

"I was thinking," said Allison, "that the search for the magnificent seven is wrong; you are one of them, just as Yul Brunner was one in the movie. So you need only 6 more; and you've got, let me see if I've got this right, the wing who can run fast, the front rower who can push hard, the scrum half, if his brother lets him play... You are half way there, three out of six."

Xolile seemed to find this very funny. "But of course it's not the absolute numbers that we want. We want to add strong individuals to the team to transform it into a winning one; but that's only half the story. We need to boost the team's quality but then we have to gel the team around a specific style of play. We'll need to rehearse over and over again a whole series of innovative manoeuvres. And we still don't have a flyhalf..." Xolile turned over the Sunday Times to the back page. They both stared at the headline: *England Rugby bad boy sued for ruining marriage*, it said.

"Jeremy, Jeremy what have you done now?" he mused.

"You don't want to reach out to him?"

He shrugged and Allison went out to the kitchen, leaving him with Leah who was staring at Xolile fixedly. On the TV there was a documentary, some part of the South African past with hundreds of kids facing a line of blue clad police.

"Why don't you have an affair with my mother?" she asked suddenly.

Xolile was thrown momentarily. "I seldom discuss my sex life with anybody… still less the daughter of a friend. But let's assume I was less retiring – how do you know I'm not sleeping with your mother?"

"Because she told me…"

"Aha… and, if I may ask, Leah, what business is it of yours?"

"I think she's lonely. My dad is never coming back and I know you like each other. I think you should date."

Xolile nodded gravely as though he were speaking to a young child. "I value your opinion but in truth I'm a driven person for whom sex is not as important as it used to be. Your mother and I start an affair – perhaps we'd happy ever after but more likely we'd complicate and mess up our working relationship, which as you know is excellent…"

Leah gave him that Meyer smile and Xolile had a sudden sense of how lovely Allison had been as a young girl. "Will you at least think about it?" she asked.

"I will. What is this programme you're watching?"

"It's an old doccie on the struggle – kids were taking on the police in Sebokeng."

"And that dance, the rush up to the police line and the retreat?"

"Come on, Xoli, where were you during the struggle? It's the toyi-toyi – I think every black kid in the country still knows how to do it…"

"I was too young, in Japan for some of those years. And the song?"

"It's some liberation song, I don't know it."

"Interesting. Very, very interesting… Ah, Allison, the chicken – can I cut it up?"

28

James Dlamini was not amused. "You want a contract for a guy who you believe will never play for the Super Rugby side? For social reasons, it seems. What is going on here? Is this guy your cousin or something? Am I being taken for a ride? Are you selling contracts?"

Xolile steeled himself to be absolutely still until his employer had run out of steam. He squeezed his Ntseku between his fingers to keep his focus.

"All that we do, all we plan to do, is to make a better performing team – so that your investment is worth more and more. The contract is for the provincial side, so not so expensive, and will only be for a year unless they want to keep him. The provincial side doesn't want to use their money for requests from the Super Rugby side so that's why I am asking you to put in the money from the Super Rugby budget. This kid, the scrumhalf, with the right training and inputs, can be a real star for the Lions. He might play for us for a decade, he's that good and that young."

James Dlamini opened his mouth to reply but Xolile cut in: "This is a sound investment I'm proposing to you."

"You can't possibly know that; we might pay this money and he gets a career ending injury in the first game..."

"Of course. This is rugby, it could happen to any of us, including me, every time we step on the field. There are no guarantees, all we can do is plan to the best of our abilities."

"Vague promises: that's all you offer me at the moment."

"Look at it another way: here's a guy who, no matter how good he is seen to be in Europe, is not going to dump us to play there because his brother is on a cheap contract with the Lions."

Dlamini signed the job offer for Chris Schwartz on his desk.

"There's something else: there's a problem with the ground, with the stadium."

"What problem?"

"It's like it's in a time warp from 30 years ago. Top rugby stadia make much more effort to be what the fans want and where people want to spend time. We need a section for families so people can bring their kids without worrying about people slopping their beer on them."

"Selling beer is a big part of our revenue, I don't want to interfere with that..."

"I think you also need a fan tent where people can drink heavily while watching the match live on a big screen. Maybe jumping castles somewhere too – and the music between plays and half time – pathetic. Don't you own a radio station? Can't you appoint a young black DJ to do the music?"

Dlamini was silent for a while. "You are not the first person to tell me these things. My problem is that I don't have anyone on staff to manage these changes. It needs someone with a bit of common sense and drive."

"Take my marketing agent, Allison Meyer. She'll look at grounds in other countries, make recommendations, with the costing of course."

"Tell her to call me then."

29

"Xolile, Jeremy Gandolfini just phoned me. We've arranged to meet at his hotel in Sandton. Can you join us?"

"How did he find you?"

"Facebook, he says. He phoned and said 'Hi! Is that the Dagger's bodyguard?'"

Xolile's laughter echoed down the phone line in her ear. "No, you meet him alone first. I want to play hard to get for a while yet."

"But what will I say to him?"

"Ag, you can wing it, easy. He'll probably try and sleep with you – tell Leah."

"What?"

30

Willie was frowning. "There's someone who I want you to meet – but I'm not sure about him myself, this maybe a waste of time…"

They drove out to a restaurant bar next to Ellis Park. Xolile asked no questions about the mystery appointment, he felt all would be revealed by the steady Willie in good time. As they strolled through the parking lot Willie suddenly said: "Do you know the new Mini Clubman?"

"It's a car, right?"

"Yeah, yeah, it's a Mini station wagon; but it looks like the makers took the old station wagon and pumped it up so every dimension is bigger."

They entered the restaurant. "So?" said Xolile, wondering where Willie was going with this. They headed to a table with one man sitting alone. Willie muttered softly "This guy has the same look – as though someone pumped him bigger…"

The 'guy' stood up as they approached. "Stefanus Lodewyk van Staden" he said as they shook hands. Xolile saw Willie's reference immediately – the man was a giant, two metres tall, powerful shoulders and trunk, arms as thick as an average man's legs…

"Do you play rugby?" he asked him.

"I played at school, at Affies." Van Staden's voice seemed to come from somewhere deep within him, a small voice given the size of the container.

"Dagger, Stefan is, was, the South African javelin record holder," said

Willie. "He can't ... um ply his trade, pursue his chosen sport anymore and he'd like to try his hand at rugby."

"Is it an injury? Why do you have to give up throwing the javelin?" asked Xolile.

Van Staden answered like a man just about to give up his friends to the police. "I was done for steroids last year – banned for life, from field events anyway."

"So why rugby then?"

"I've been a professional sportsman for almost ten years – I have no trade, no future, no way of earning a living anymore. I thought with my size I could maybe come back into professional rugby?" He ended with a questioning note to his voice.

"And he played lock at school" put in Willie. "Look, Dagger, there seems to be two elements here: firstly and most importantly, can he perform and contribute to the team? He would be another player in his late twenties learning the game for the first time, first time at the highest level anyway..."

"And the other element?"

Willie looked uncomfortable. Xolile guessed he didn't even want to use the words 'anabolic steroids'.

"There's the scandal element as well, of his, his penalty. People are going to say we're building a team of crooks, of cheats."

"I don't see that as a big thing for us – no more steroids right, Clubman?"

The javelin thrower was a bit nonplussed by the use of his new nickname. "Uh… no I'll never do those again if I'm playing rugby."

"Clubman, then let's give you a trial, a three month contract off season and see if we can fit you in to the team. Do you agree, Willie?"

He nodded and handshakes sealed the deal.

31

Allison wore a smart business outfit for her meeting with Gandolfini, the skirt a touch short the jacket showing off a hint of bosom. As she left her house she suddenly changed her mind and flung on her standard jeans and tee shirt.

She waited in the lobby of the Radison Blu Hotel in Sandton where he had told her he was staying. He was exactly seven minutes late. He was, however, freshly shaved, neatly dressed and seemingly sober.

"Hi hi" he said, kissing her cheek European style, "so we didn't speak in Cape Town really. Are you The Dagger's girlfriend?"

"No" she said shortly, "I'm his grandmother."

He laughed and they ordered lime and sodas.

Jeremy got straight down to business. "Look, I messed up with The Dagger that time. I'd had a bit to drink, should have been more humble, I know. But I really want to play for the Lions, I want to show what I am capable of on the rugby field. I've got talent, even the Dagger can see that but I keep on messing up, keep on letting myself and my teams down. I don't know why I can't keep on the straight and narrow…"

In a rare moment for Allison she felt both contempt for his little boy routine and an enormous power within her. Suddenly she felt she knew what Xolile would say to Gandolfini if he were there…

"It's because you lack the discipline to make the most of your talents. The Dagger is putting a world beating team together, a team that's committed to each other and the tasks ahead. He doubts that you have the necessary resolve to be a part of that – and so do I."

Allison steeled herself for what she imagined would be a rage response from him but he was still doing the little boy thing: "I want that discipline, I think I can respond to a great leader, I need this job…."

"We heard about your court case – is that why you've come back to the Lions?" In her mind, Allison saw herself as a boxer, pounding her opponent unmercifully.

"No, I was going to see you anyway, well, yes, the case and these damned lawyers does make it important for me to earn a good living, but no…"

Allison tuned out as he burbled along. There must be a way to hook him in and bring the meeting to a conclusion with a tryout for the Lions, surely that's the most that Xolile would give him at this stage?

Gandolfini was now into the prepared phase of his pitch – how if he were just given a chance he could do wonders for the Lions and be a model player.

She interrupted him. "If you are absolutely determined that the nonsense that has dogged your career until now is over then maybe I can persuade the Dagger to give you a month by month contract…"

"Month by month? Nobody does that anymore!"

"It's month by month for the first six months or nothing as far as I'm concerned. The Dagger might have his own view on this but it seems to me that if you fuck up in the first six months we would want you to just leave without having months of negotiations with your lawyers about how much you get paid out. What do you say?"

106

"I'm in" he said and flashed his radiant smile at her.

She phoned Xolile who told her tell him to report to Willie at Ellis Park the next Monday for contracting and planning his off season training.

Their business done, Allison rose to leave.

"Have dinner with me, Allie." He put his hand on her arm as if to detain her. Allison hated the fact that she liked his soft warm hand on her skin. She shook him off, but gently.

"That would be completely inappropriate" she told him primly.

"Hey I'm new in town what am I going to do for the next three days?"

"Read a book, catch up on the movies on circuit, keep out of bars and clubs." Allison shook his hand and left before, she said to herself, she began to see his side of his isolation.

32

On a balmy summer's afternoon in December, Xolile dropped in on the additional training camp – the magnificents plus four players undergoing long term rehabilitation for injury.

The biokinetecist and the fitness training coach ambled over to him.

"How're the lads doing?"

"Reasonably" said Gerhard, the fitness coach. "Best of the lot is Mahlangu – he can pass and catch the ball ok now, we're working on his tackling. He shows a lot of heart... The new guy, Clubman, he can bench press an average bus, he's simply enormous. He's tall of course so the lineout jumping is improving...."

"And the lineouts generally?" asked Xolile.

"Well we've got that stringbean from the under 20's, Smith, and the big loosies can take lineout ball as they did last year. Then Clubman will have to do what Jan did for us in previous years – take front ball regularly."

"Call him over," said Xolile, "I want to ask him something."

"Chimmy is putting on weight but only 3 kgs so far; Jason the scrumhalf we've working on his pass, trying to put a few more metres on it."

"Yeah, I think that's important. But even more important is his speed at clearing from the rucks."

"Hard to practice that out of a match situation. We all play sevens every afternoon but of course there are few rucks in that format..."

"Lock him away for the weekend watching Aaron Smith's last four games – that's what we want from him…"

Clubman trotted over. He and Xolile exchanged minor pleasantries about training, accommodation and transport.

"Hey, Clubman, as a javelin thrower how far can you throw a rugby ball?"

"I dunno really… I've never gone for distance before."

"Let's try it."

They gave him a rugby ball on the touchline and Xolile took up a position about 30 metres infield. "Go!" he shouted at Clubman. With a strange action for a rugby player, Clubman wound up briefly and let the ball go with a perfect spiral action.

"Wow" said Xolile quietly to himself as the ball flew at least ten metres over his head.

He took up a position further away and started twenty metres further back so that he could run on to the ball at speed. They practiced another dozen or so times and then Jim took over from Xolile. Gerhard and Jeremy were nodding sagely.

"Very nice move" said Gerhard, "you can surprise a few teams with that. Straight from a lineout or ruck to the wings – you and Jim can be in business."

"Keep him practicing that throw – it's probably a move we can't use more than once a game but, as you say, could be a big surprise each time. How's Gandolfini doing?"

Jeremy answered slowly. "Ja, he's ok I suppose, certainly no problems with discipline or attitude, loads of talent of course…"

"But? What?"

"Guy says he's lonely. He doesn't want to drink anymore at night but what else is there to do in a foreign town?"

Xolile nodded. "We're going to try and fix that soon."

As he headed back to his car a figure detached himself from the handful of watchers and waved him down. Xolile knew from the way he walked and the set of his shoulders that he was a front ranker, either current or past.

"Putting the untouchables through their paces?" the Coloured man said by way of opening.

"Yup," said Xolile, "you want to join? Who did you kill?"

What had been intended as a flip remark had a considerable effect on the stranger. He visibly blanched and almost stuttered a reply: "You know who I am?"

"No idea" said Xolile, "but I think we'd better talk in the office."

33

They shook hands. "Cecil Oliphant" said the man.

Something triggered in Xolile's memory. He knew that name, but in what context?

"Tell me your story" he said to Oliphant.

After a slow start the man poured out his recent history without inflection or emotion:

Four years ago I was playing for the Bulls and we went to a party at my brother in law's in Pretoria East. I had a few drinks, maybe four or five over about 6 hours so I was probably legally intoxicated but not drunk. At exactly five minutes past midnight I was stopped by two traffic policemen, both, as I found out later, from Bronkhorstspruit. They were doing a night stop in central Pretoria picking up bribes, whatever they could wring from the mostly drunk drivers out at night.

They stopped me and requested a bribe or they said they would take me to the police station for a Breathalyzer. I refused to go and I wouldn't pay the bribe and things began to get ugly. I got out of my car and one of them swung at me, a rubbish sort of warning punch.

I should tell you that I'm not much of a fighter, don't really have a good attitude or even much of a punch. But since I started playing rugby, because I'm big, I became good at picking people up and throwing them down. In rugby and in the rest of my life that has always been enough to put an end to any physical encounters.

So the first cop punches me and I pick him up and throw him away. He lands a metre or two from me but he's fine, he gets straight back up to his feet.

Then the second cop pulls out his pistol and I think, oh oh, here's trouble. So I grab his gun hand, and hold it up and at the same time I get my other hand under his trunk and lift him up. Then I throw him down just like the first one. But perhaps because I hold his gun hand up in the air he has no balance and he lands on a pole nearby head first.

The pathologist told me later that he suffered an immediate skull fracture and a massive bleed into his brain. So he falls to the ground and within seconds he starts convulsing. The other cop and I rush to him, we neither of us have any idea what to do. The other cop starts stroking his brow and saying 'Tula, Petrus, tula' over and over.

I can't remember what I did but on the video camera you can see that I was crying, weeping like a child. Within five minutes, again from the video footage, the guy is dead.

"Video footage?" asks Xolile.

Central Pretoria has CCTV. These two morons from Bronkhorstspruit are shaking down punters in the city centre not realizing that their own service is recording them.

So you can guess what happens next. I'm arrested on a charge of first degree murder, later changed to culpable homicide. The newspapers go to town on me – you can imagine, another steroid rage rugby racial homicide. My family takes it badly, many of my relatives still don't talk to me, my wife leaves me, ok we had problems before, but this was the final straw for her.

But the case against me is weak: the CCTV footage shows these two guys breaking the law repeatedly over the previous couple of hours; the cop threw the first punch, pulled a gun for no clear reason.

The dead man's family went to the press, Archbishop Tutu, the South African Council of Churches. They accused me of being a cold blooded murderer. Then the police told them that even the culpable homicide charge probably wouldn't wash. The lawyers got together and I paid the family off – case closed. Or so I thought. But my career as a professional rugby player was over. No Super team would touch me.

So now I work as a security guard and play amateur rugby for Pirates....

"And you want from me?" asked Xolile.

"I want to play for the Lions. I want to resuscitate my career."

"Playing club rugby did you ever scrum against this Zimbo, Chimmy, plays for Pirates?"

"Yeah, I've played him twice this season."

Wordlessly, Xolile hauled out his cell phone and called Chimmy. Oliphant listened to one side of the conversation.

"How's it going? ... Good, good. Listen quick question: did you ever scrum against a guy called Cecil Oliphant? Yes... What did you think of him? Really? OK thanks, we'll speak again soon."

Xolile shut off the phone and he and Oliphant stared at each other for a while.

"What did he say?"

"He said you were the best player he'd ever scrummed against..."

Oliphant's face crinkled into a smile.

"Don't get too excited – Chimmy is a good player, potentially a great player, but his exposure to the highest levels of front rank play is limited. You might be his best but that's doesn't mean you're the best in the country."

Oliphant looked crestfallen. "But," continued Xolile, "I'll have to speak to the coach but I think you might do nicely for us. However, you have to face what's coming if you play Super Rugby – every dumb forward in the world is going to remind you of your past every opportunity they get. You've got to wear this incident with pride, not shame."

"And how exactly do I do that?"

"We'll send you for a couple of sessions with the team psychologist. And you'll use your new nick name immediately. Welcome to the Lions, Killer…"

34

Xolile sat in his favourite Japanese restaurant, surrounded by the magnificent six. Despite his best efforts, it was a sombre affair – Chimmy and Jason were born agains and didn't drink; Gandolfini was doing his impression of good behaviour – basically sulking and not drinking ostentatiously; Clubman and the Killer were nursing single beers without enthusiasm; only Jim seemed to have the semblance of a good time, he at least enjoyed the foreign food....

Xolile smsed Allison: *I'm dying here. Where is she?*

5 minutes, she smsed back.

When Allison and Noluthando entered the restaurant it was as though a ray of sunshine had entered with them – suddenly the whole place looked brighter.

Allison pulled up a chair between Clubman and Killer. "I'm Allison, I don't think we've met. I work with the Dagger." This left only one seat for Noluthando – next to Gandolfini.

Xolile ate his tempura with little enthusiasm for his group. When he had finished he glanced at Gandolfini and Noluthando and saw them giggling conspiratorially.

Allison gave up conversation with Clubman and sat next to him.

"They must be good rugby players because socially they're a bit inept" she murmured. "And thanks for the contact with Ellis Park. I think we'll propose doing what the Sharks and Reds do with their stadiums, family orientated."

35

Willie was hesitant on the phone. "I am not disturbing am I?"

"What is it, Willie?"

"I don't want to worry you about this, it probably is my job but ... Gandolfini hasn't been to practice for three days. And his cell phone is on voice mail."

"I'll go around to his flat now – maybe it's nothing, maybe he's just been hijacked and held prisoner for three days…"

"That's a joke, right?"

"Yes, Willie."

"Oh and, uh, Dagger? He's been trying, he really has…"

"I'm sure… I'll get back to you."

When Xolile knocked on the door of Gandolfini's apartment there was a sense of there being someone inside but it took several knocks and bangs before the door opened. Noluthando appeared at the door dressed only in a sheet.

"Hi, Dagger" she said with an insouciant air. He followed her into the apartment, noting with only mild regret her luminous grace as the sheet flirted with her body. The apartment smelt of sex and sweat but Xolile was relieved that there were no signs of alcohol anywhere. Jeremy came out of the toilet in a pair of shorts and embraced Noluthando.

"You've missed practice for three days," Xolile said to him

accusingly.

"No, just today, surely? What day is it today, anyway?"

Xolile rounded on Noluthando and spoke to her in Xhosa. "**Imel' ukuba nguwe osincedisayo kodwa ngok' uyalahla!**" , meaning "you are supposed to be helping keep him on the road not distract him; if he doesn't practice don't give him any sex, do you hear?"

"Oh Dagger! We are just so in love…"

Xolile spoke to both of them in English: "What you both don't seem to understand is that everything depends on Jeremy giving his absolute best to the team, including showing up for every practice, every meeting, no matter how unimportant it seems to you both. How he performs is another matter – but for Jeremy it is essential that he gives of his utmost. The way his personality works he is good at everything only when he is good at rugby, do you understand, Thando? Otherwise everything goes – the job, your new relationship, everything is under threat if he starts a downward spiral…"

Gandolfini nodded in agreement. "Yeah, yeah, you're right, Dagger. I'm sorry man, it won't happen again."

"Take tomorrow off and be back at practice on Monday" Xolile told him, "but this is your last chance."

As they were thanking him Xolile said to Noluthando in Xhosa "**Ungasidanisi sonke sithembele kuwe** ", meaning "The whole team is relying on you – don't let us down."

36

The weeks sped by and before any of the Magnificent Seven could imagine, it was the full team pre-season training programme. The first Saturday evening after the commencement of full training, Willie and Xolile hosted a dinner evening for the whole squad, coaches, trainers, and Allison and the girls. He told Allison he had prepared extensively for the evening – he wanted, he said, everyone to be on the same page after the dinner.

The coach spoke first: "Our aim is to be the best rugby side in the world, to win the Super 15 competition, but it is not *just* that – in the team we want slowly to build the spirit, the commitment to each other. Some of us might well be the best players in the world in our positions, but most of us are not. We are a team without current national players. We seek to build a team that is much, much stronger than simply adding our individual capacities together, a team that the other Super clubs fear, not because we are the Springboks in waiting, but because we combine and play off each other more effectively than other teams.

"It's like laying bricks – a brick is just a brick; you add another to it you have two bricks. But if you stack up the bricks suddenly you have something completely different – you have a wall. Dagger and I have had many discussions about how we might achieve this, how we might build a wall. We've discussed it just the two of us just because we've both been around off season but obviously we are looking for ideas from all of you."

It was past ten when Xolile rose to his feet to signal it was time for his talk. The food was gone, alcohol still being poured down throats, the magician had finished his show and Andile had done an introductory word of thanks.

"Friends, teammates, colleagues, comrades… greetings. I have several issues that I want to run through with you. Firstly, there has been a bit in the media about the so called Magnificent Seven – these were the players who were contracted during the off season. I want to make sure that you all understand that there is no two tiers of players at the Lions of 2015. There is no special group called the magnificents who are entitled to special conditions or to play automatically. No. What the newspapers call the magnificents are merely players we've added in key positions. In addition, some of the magnificents have little rugby experience – Jim and Clubman, for example. Our plan is not that the magnificents are automatic first choices, rather we will introduce them as subs one at a time in the first 5 or 6 matches.

"The second rumour I want to speak to is the claim that we want to turn the Lions into a black team. We certainly want the team to have a blacker look and mix of players, surely we all support that aim?"

He looked around the room until several players nodded.

"But our aim is to build the best non national team in the world, irrespective of where players come from. You can see that the six players we've added are demographically neutral – 2 black players, 2 coloured, 1 from another country and 1 local white. Our aim is primarily to win, not to transform."

He paused. "I am aware that the black players have formed a, what do you call it, a caucus? I see no harm in this. I am not a member, as captain I think I should be outside of groups. But let's do this in an open way. Can someone in the caucus speak to the aims and the methods of the group?"

Andile spoke: "It is very clear that for black players that are part of the team we often feel like we are … visitors, perhaps guests would be a better word. The history, the culture, the Afrikaans weigh heavily on us black players. In addition, and I'm not talking about Willie here, we often think the coaches are a bit uncomfortable with us – any lapse in form and we get booted out whereas we see white players getting motivational stuff from the coaches, the psychologist and so on. So the caucus is really just to provide a, a soft landing I think it's called, for new black players and a support structure if things don't go well. That, and to take forward any grievances the young players might have…."

"Any objections?"

Karel Buys raised his hand. "I understand what Andi has said and sympathise; but do we want to maintain racial separation? I'm referring to the roommates' question. Usually the black guys room together when there are only two or four – now that there are more of them it's going to look more like a statement when we have, say, four black rooms and ten white ones. I propose that the rooms are consciously mixed so that we can be one team. Thank you."

Andile was on his feet right away. "In principle I'm with Karel but there are other realities. Because of the isolation I referred to, when a new black player comes into the team he is usually mentored by an older black hand. That includes sharing rooms. I would be very opposed to enforced integration just for appearances' sake."

A fairly lively debate ensued. Allison was surprised to see that despite the rather formal nature of the evening, players were confident to speak from the floor, often interrupting each other good naturedly.

Eventually Xolile called a halt to this issue. "I'm sort of with Andile on this – I don't think a blanket rule will do. But at the same time we don't want to have two squads in effect, where all the black players room together and all the white ones room together. Let's leave it to the black caucus to handle things sensitively."

He paused, then said as an aside: "You know this is a funny country – if I had told my grandfather when he was alive in the 1990s that twenty years later we'd have a debate where the white players call for integration and the black players want segregation I'm sure he would not have believed it… But anyway, moving on:

"Firstly, we know that all South African teams struggle to win away from home. So the question is why is that and what can we do to increase our chances of winning away?"

Answers flew in thick and fast: we're unused to the grounds, the fans intimidate us, the fans intimidate the referees so that it feels like we're playing 16 men, the hotels are not like home, the food is shit, the beer is too warm, the beer is too cold…

"OK, OK," said Xolile, "but which of these can we intervene in, which can we change to our advantage?"

Inane suggestions ("fly our own beer in") were dispensed with in short order. It was eventually Jan Wessels, the wing who said: "We need to disarm the crowds when we tour Aus and New Zealand."

"Exactly!" said Xolile. "And I now believe I made a terrible mistake in baiting the Crusaders fans last year – Mike Chisholm was right when he told me I was a fool. We can't disarm the fans by taking the piss out of them, we've got to somehow make them like us, or at least tolerate us. How can we do this?"

Allison thought that Xolile had already plans for this but he took comments from the floor, managed conflicting thoughts, discounted the truly outlandish, and finally pushed the audience to a consensus. This took close to an hour but at the end of it he had on a flip board chart, five points.

Play with greater flair than other South African touring teams

Train at local schools while on tour

Drink at local bars

Hold coaching clinics for school kids

Always be generous to local players and fans

They all looked at the list with some satisfaction. "Anyone got anything else?"

Hesitantly, Allison put up her hand.

"You all know Allison? She is a journalist, got me my towel sponsorship and has done various things for the team. At the moment she has been employed by Ellis Park to redesign it into a more family friendly ground. She'll probably interview some of you later in the year."

Allison said: "If you tour several cities in Australasia it would probably be a good idea to support a charity theme that can be found in every town. I would suggest something involving children, either orphaned or disabled, something where celebrities like yourselves" at this several players hooted with laughter at being called celebrities, "No, if you live in Perth, say, you guys are celebrities. Do you think Lady Gaga goes to Perth?"

More laughter. "Any proposals on the charity then?" asked Xolile.

Jason put up his hand. "My cousin is in a wheel chair – she was born with Spina Bifida, it's a disease where the spinal cord doesn't close in the mother's womb and then you can't walk properly. And you find kids with this thing everywhere in the world."

"Good, Jason. Everyone ok with Spina Bifida as our special interest? Fine, then. Allison maybe you can do a little article for the newspaper, perhaps interview Jason as well and we'll formally announce that Spina Bifida will be our project for this year because one of our players has family afflicted by it."

"Then we are also planning a series of new drills and set moves – original ones that might take some teams by surprise. Willie will be running through those at practice and we plan to unveil them at different matches through the season.

"Andile and I are working on a war dance, something unusual that will attract quite a bit of media. We'll show you that when we've got a decent song to go with it. We're in negotiation with a dance teacher..." He had to pause as hoots of derision and laughter went round the room. "... with a dance teacher called Lisa who has ideas about how our war dance might look. You'll hear more about this as the season continues."

"And finally: we want to use the reserves a bit differently to everyone else. Willie and I believe that we would be more effective, particularly late in the match where the game is often won or lost, if everyone knew at the start of the match who is going to be replaced by whom. Accordingly we want to try this scheme: at 55 minutes, irrespective of the state of the match, six reserves come on – three front rowers and three loose forward/locks. In this way we hope to deliver a real punchy last quarter in every match. At the same time the loosies and the props need hold nothing in reserve after half time because they know they will be replaced after fifteen minutes. We hope that, in time, we'll develop specialist reserves who come on only to be explosive in last bit of the match. Let's see how that develops."

Comments from the floor were invited and various players spoke about their commitment to the team and hope for new season. Finally, at midnight, drunk and happy, the team dispersed to their homes.

37

Allison and Xolile sat in the Japanese restaurant. He had just finished reading her proposal for the re-engineering of Ellis Park, based largely on what went on at the Sharks in Durban and the Reds in Brisbane.

"Excellent!" said Xolile as he handed the document back to her, "Sorry you couldn't get a free overseas trip out of this... but the things you've proposed here should make a difference to how the stadium feels for the fans."

"Thanks," she said, munching on a piece of cauliflower in a batter, "season starts in two weeks – you guys ready? Are you anxious? Do you do anxiety?"

He laughed. "We're not nearly ready. And yes I am both anxious and full of anticipation."

"I think it's time to get back on the twitter round – you've not posted for months."

"Advise me on what to say – I'm too busy trying to hold everyone together to be creative…"

He tapped his Ntseku against his teeth and they looked into each others' eyes for a while.

"What is it?" he asked her finally.

"No nothing, it's just…. I really enjoy working with you guys, it's given me a drive and interest that I thought I'd lost."

38

Lisa, the modern dance teacher, was a picture in a long pony tail and bright leotard.

As an introduction, the captain, she couldn't remember his name, had said: "These guys are fitter than your average class, so drive them hard. They'll be complainers, though, and will have a horror of anything they regard as effeminate."

An hour later they had been through the routine several times and everyone, Lisa included, was sweating freely.

"And again: from the top. Feel the music, you've been in a dungeon for years, you can hardly believe that you're free. Suck in the free air."

"But it is in German," complained Buys.

"Never the mind the language, savour the freedom after so long. That's it. Now up straight, look to the heavens, yes, now your song, loud, give it everything you've got... Now wheel, your opponents are that wall at the end. Go right up to them and show them you're free, give them the song, in their faces. Not bad, not bad at all..."

PART THREE

39

As the new Super Rugby season approached, a sense of anticipation seemed to grip the traditional Lions fans, or that's what Allison told Xolile anyway, judged on the twitter traffic.

Typical amongst the comments was one from J. Louw of Roodepoort: *At last! A winning Lions team – I can't wait*

The first match of the season against the Cheetahs in Bloemfontein – even the home town supporters said the Lions should win easily. Playing in Bloem wasn't the same as playing in Joburg at Ellis Park but it was a damn sight easier than playing at Eden Park in New Zealand, said Andile.

The Cheetahs had lost 6 of their best players to France, the UK and the Bulls. They were, according to local rugby scribes, a shadow of their former selves.

Allison had to attend a school gala for Rosemary, who despite the family's disinterest in the sport, was turning out to be a good swimmer. Allison's ex-husband referred to her as the Michelle Phelps of Parkhurst – and so the whole family was surprised when they turned to the rugby scores later to discover that the Cheetahs had thumped the Lions by 30 points to 18.

The performance of the Lions was nothing short of shameful – knock ons, missed tackles, mindless aggression leading to a string of penalties and one yellow card. The Lions had been in the game until the yellow card at minute 61 – then the score was only 16 to 13 to the

Bloem side. But the Lions conceded two tries, fourteen points, while Kobus Boshoff was in the sin bin. Everyone had been below par though – even Xolile had spilled the ball in the first half when the tryline had been open.

The only bright element was Jason. Picked on the bench, the incumbent scrumhalf had injured his knee after only twenty minutes play and Jason had played the better part of an hour – pretty well, Xolile thought.

He had a particular style in a match which no one in the Lions had been aware of until today – he talked nonstop through the game. He talked to his teammates, his opponents, the referee, the water boys and at one time he seemed to get into an altercation with a spectator. The thing was that although he talked a lot he spoke in a monotonous high pitch with a pronounced Northern Cape accent. Xolile wasn't even sure what language it was although he thought it was Afrikaans.

"Jason played well," said Andile as they trudged to their cars. Four of the Magnificents had been on the bench but only Jason got game time. Xolile thought Willie didn't want to sully them by playing them in a disastrous first match.

"Yeah he did, didn't he?" answered Xolile, "but we never noticed in training how he talked all the time, even when he's passing. What does he say?"

"He seems to mutter loudly. Most of the time nobody can make out what he's saying. But he called the Cheetahs scrumhalf an 'etter' – the guy didn't like it but none of us know what it means."

"And what's the news from Noluthando? Gandolfini still on the straight and narrow?"

"Thando says they're great – still in love and spend a lot of time shopping together. And he looks sharp in practice."

"Maybe we can blood him at the next match, what do you think?"

"I think it's time but let's not even use the word blood. You know he's going to be a target when other teams know he's our secret weapon?"

"One of our secret weapons – aren't you the other, the hooker with a smart arse word for every occasion?"

They chuckled companionably as they got into their cars.

The Star, 17th February 2015.

Some of the Lions players paid an unexpected visit to the Moshe Lewin Home for the Physically Disabled in Eldorado Park yesterday. In the photo alongside vice-captain Andile Phike, accompanied by five other stars, passes a rugby ball to twelve year old Elphas Gumede, who has been in a wheelchair since birth. Said Elphas "Andile has always been my hero and it's great to actually meet him in person. If I wasn't in a wheelchair I think I would be a rugby player like him."

The Lions were collectively surprised to find out that one of their new players, Jason Schwartz, has a family member with a congenital condition called Spina Bifida, the same condition that Elphas was born with.

Says Phike: "Once we started meeting kids like Elphas we all immediately said we want to use our public image to raise awareness of this disease. We'll always be available for any fundraising, fetes, disabled sports days – you name it – for people born with Spina Bifida. We know that this is a condition that requires lots of resources if individuals are to have the best chance of having a good, fulfilling life. That's why we plan to visit homes like this in Australia and New Zealand while we are on tour. Perhaps we can even get some ideas for back home."

Allison Meyer

Andile sms ed Allison: *Congratulations! You almost made me sound intelligent.*

Allison replied: *You are intelligent, you big idiot!*

40

Jason's brother, Chris, asked Willie and Xolile to go through the previous week's video footage with him. Reluctantly, Xolile agreed – they had already watched the video as a team and he thought there was little point in repeating anything just for Chris. As an afterthought he invited Andile and Jeremy as well.

They sat in the video viewing room at the stadium. Jeremy sat in the front, talking away to Jason while Chris had one those laser pointers that he shone now and then on the screen to draw their attention to one thing or another.

Xolile had hardly heard Chris say much, and what he did say was, like his brother, open to interpretation. So it was a few minutes before he realised that Chris was talking in English in a very comprehensible way.

"You see," Chris said to Jason, "this is good ball, attacking ball, you need to get it out to the backs or the loose forwards immediately before the defence reforms. But there, you take a step and then decide to pass to Gandolfini. That's too slow, man. You must know before you get to the ruck where the ball is going. Then it's in and pass in one movement, yes?"

Jeremy and Willie were nodding and Jason was saying "Ja, ja I see it now..."

"And here: your worst moment in the game, a kick directly into touch. If I was a loose forward playing with you I would have moered you right then. The forwards battle to get forward and then you give the ball away twenty metres further back... it's kak play, man, there's no other word for it."

"And here again: but that's a better pass from you. You know you play with a flyhalf who likes to take the ball flat or deep – that's unusual but good for the team. You have to know this guy like intimately, you have to know what he's thinking before he thinks it, right?"

Jeremy and Jason eyed each other speculatively. Neither seemed that thrilled to become each other's best friend. Xolile wondered idly if there were two rugby players on the planet more dissimilar than those two.

"I think you should room together when we tour," said Willie, "try and build a bond between you..."

"And here," Chris went on, pausing the film, "the opposing eighth man comes around the scrum evades our loosies and he's in your face. This happens only a couple times a game but then he's yours. You have to bring him down hard and wait for support from the forwards. You have to etter him without hesitation, bang, bring him down and lie on him or he will release the ball and there's an easy try for the opposition..."

"And here, you've got to tell the forwards which way to go – the pod is standing to the left of the ruck but that's where the defence is strong. You should have told them to go right before you get the ball in your hands. In this situation you've got to boss them, that's your job, right?"

And so it went. At the end of the session they all agreed they would do the same after each match they played but only Chris, Willie and the two half backs would attend.

As they walked out Andile said to Xolile "Who would have thought?

Chris is like some idiot savant of the rugby field...."

"Yeah. I'm going to ask Willie to send him on a coach's course. He might still have a career with the Lions."

41

The lead up to the Lions second match of the season, against the Stormers at Newlands in Cape Town, was marked by large amounts of comment, in the orthodox media and in social media. Most of the rugby journalists saw the Lions as continuing the previous years' seamless underperformance.

Cape Town had seen a slow drizzle for seven days; the city and the Newlands rugby grounds were soaked in that Mediterranean-climate way that leant the impression that under the grass there was half a metre of water and mud. Nevertheless, the ground was close to full and the crowd was good naturedly hostile.

In the change room of the Lions the mood was tense, anxious even. Players paced around slapping each other on the back, high fiving, banging shoulders. Xolile wondered if the change rooms for women rugby players were very different – was kissing and hugging more the norm?

Jason was in the starting fifteen and so was Jeremy Gandolfini. On the bench, due to come on for the last 20 minutes, Chimmy and Clubman waited to debut. Despite the constant rain and the heavy conditions under foot, the first half went well for the Lions. They trotted into the change room at the half time break 13 to 9 ahead.

Willie was business like in his half time talk: "Keep on doing the basics right; kick shallow and follow up. Don't slack off on your tackling."

Fresh jerseys were distributed and the planned substitutions twenty minutes into the second half repeated.

The Lions trotted out onto the field full of confidence – and simply disintegrated. Within ten minutes two players were in the bin – including Xolile for knocking down the ball in a try saving effort. Playing for seven minutes with only thirteen men was an effective knockout blow to the Lions – two converted tries to the Stormers ended the game as a contest. Chimmy and the Clubman made their debuts as planned in the last quarter. Within five minutes of arriving on the field Clubman was provoked into a fight with the Stormers hooker and sent off. Finishing with a man down, yet another try was gifted to the Stormers to give them a comfortable victory.

The interviewer after the match was determined not to give Xolile an easy ride about the Lions' second defeat. He also didn't want to call him Dagger but couldn't do the click in his name.

"X, you and the coach repeatedly promised that there would be a new Lions team on display this year. So far it looks pretty much like business as usual for the team. What did you hope would be done better?"

"Well, Keith, although we've got no wins as yet it's still early days – the Super 15 is not lost in February. Although we are disappointed by the disciplinary penalties we incurred today it is a vastly improved performance compared to the debacle against the Cheetahs last week. So we feel we are steadily improving and the wins will start coming soon."

"When you say 'soon' do you mean that you are going to win the next match?" persisted the interviewer.

"Of course we'll beat the Bulls at Loftus next week," replied Xolile with a confidence he didn't for a moment feel.

"What about Jeremy Gandolfini? Did you expect more from him?"

"I certainly did. I expected him to make up for all the deficiencies in the team and run us to victory with 13 men on the field. I'm extremely disappointed he didn't do that."

"You joke about that but there was a lot of preseason talk about the new signings, the Magnificent Seven some called them, and how they were going to revolutionise the Lions and its playing style. Only a few of them have had game time – do you still see them as game breakers, as match winners?"

"This is a similar question to the Gandolfini one. The new signings were to boost our playing reserves and to bring in some selected skills. They were never going to function apart from our team's commitment to play good rugby and to win more than we lose. So far as a team we haven't deserved to win a match and haven't done so. It's no more the new signings fault than it is the rest of ours…"

42

The team was in the change room when Karel Buys came in from the shower area.

"Hey, Andi," he called to Andile, "come and have a look at Jason."

Andile trotted off back into the showers and came back chuckling.

"Something funny?" asked Xolile.

"Yeah, very. There's another surprising thing about Jason. He's very large in a good department..."

Just then Jason came wandering in to the changing area wearing a towel. He started frittling in his carry bag, pulling out items to wear and cosmetics, laying them carefully on the counter in front of him. He pulled out a pair of underpants and whisked his towel off with a bit of a flourish. Giggles, hearty laughter and a whistle broke out in the change room. Jason suddenly realised everyone was looking at him.

"What?" he said. "What? What?"

Everyone was laughing now and Andile took pity on the bemused Jason.

"Jason, my buddy, you've finally got a nickname. Inyoka, Slang, welcome to the team, Snake..."

Other players came up to him and embraced him, high fived him. People tried out his nick name. For a while it seemed that 'Slang' – Afrikaans for snake – might win out but by the time they had all left for home 'Snake' was his nick name for ever.

43

Allison collected a series of the cleverest tweets going around and asked Xolile if he wanted to see them or not.

"Of course," he said, "if you play the game you have to take the bruises."

Selected tweets:

- *Lions without a bite; dagger without a point?*

- *I'll be at Loftus Saturday to watch the magnificently underwhelming Lions*

- *The Lions will dag their own graves…*

- *What language does the Lions new scrumhalf speak – latin?*

- *Where's Gandolfini – having his picture taken?*

- *Didn't the Dagger used to be pretty fast and score tries? His form has plummeted since he became captain.*

The next game was in Pretoria against the Bulls. There was a good crowd in but not full and an air of anticipation clothed the stadium. The number one half back combination, Jason and Jeremy, and Clubman started the game. Chimmy was on the bench but the rest of the Magnificents were not to be involved.

The Bulls, also promising much in the new season, had retreated to their traditional massive forward and power game. The Bulls began to boss the Lions in the scrums and then in pick and drive moves. They milked penalties and kicked them over and just on half time kicked a penalty for the corner and from the line out mauled the ball over the line for the first try of the game. At half time the Lions trailed by 16 points to 6.

At the start of the second half the Lions tighthead prop went orr with a knee injury and was replaced by Chimmy.

A few minutes later the next scrum was called after a forward pass by the Lions. Chimmy's power was immediately apparent and the Bulls loose head lost his bind and the scrum splintered. The referee, a South African by the name of Eland, blew the whistle for the end of the scrum and a penalty. The Lions forwards slapped Chimmy on the back – until they realised that the penalty had gone against them. "Boring in," said the ref laconically and pointed at Chimmy.

Much worse was to follow. Three more scrums ended in the apparent destruction of the Bulls loosehead side only for the Lions tighthead to be penalised. The Bulls lead had gone out to twenty points now. At the last scrum Chimmy was given a yellow card for repeated infringements at the scrum. Xolile came close to the Eland. He later told Allison he did it deliberately so their conversation would be relayed to the TV audience. "You've got this all wrong" he told him, "our tight head is destroying the opposition. The penalties should all have gone the other way."

"Well that's not the way I see it" said the ref. "I see a scrum that is being disrupted by a smaller man not scrumming straight."

"I accept that's your opinion. But it's wrong. Can't you get an opinion from your assistants, the linesmen over there?"

"I do not need any assistance from the linesmen nor from you," said Eland.

"But you are ruining the game for every one – look at the Bulls players, when you penalise us they laugh because they know as well as we do that you know nothing about scrums."

Eland turned instantly furious. "I won't tolerate insolence from any of the players. You, particularly as captain, should know better." He held up a yellow card for the TV cameras to see. Xolile trudged off to the sin bin – his second offence in three weeks.

Another lineout to the Lions and Clubman was ready. Most teams had a complex series of calls, usually a series of numbers to indicate which player was going to be lifted to receive the ball. Andile claimed this was a relic from another era when lifting in the lineout was against the law. These days lifting had turned lineouts into a pretty secure source of ball for the team throwing in. Accordingly he had announced that he would be throwing the ball in according to the following pattern: Clubman, Clubman, Smith, Clubman, Clubman, Smith…

Smith was the under 21 lock, a stringbean who Willie said would be as good as John Eales in three or four years. Everyone called him *Lange*, Afrikaans for 'long one'. The first lineout throw went to Clubman. The front rank and loose forward supporting him lifted him by the thighs and he soared into the air to claim the lobbed throw in from Andile – and knocked it on.

Five minutes later the Lions got another throw in but the lifters messed up the timing and the ball flew over Clubman's head.

"Keep on throwing to him until he takes a ball then go back to your pattern," Xolile instructed Andile.

The next lineout was in fact taken by Clubman but was not in straight.

"My bad, sorry," Andile muttered to the team.

The next lineout Clubman fluffed the take and Jason got the ball and a loose forward in his face at the same time.

"Carry on" said Xolile.

"This could get ugly," Andile warned.

The next lineout Clubman knocked on again. Sections of the crowd were now openly laughing at the Lions lineout shambles.

"Ek kannie" he said to Xolile, I can't do it...

"Oh yes you can," Xolile told him, "we'll keep going until you pull one down."

The final whistle was seconds away when the Lions got a penalty for a high tackle. They kicked for the corner and the lineout was only five metres from the tryline. The crowd near the corner blew raspberries and jeered at Andile as he set up for the lineout.

The ball went in, the front ranks lifted, Clubman went up, knocked the ball backwards but grabbed it again while he was still aloft, juggled it in various positions around his body ("I thought he was trying to hide the ball in his jersey for a while" Andile later told Allison.)

But as he slid down his supports he had the ball in two hands. He let out a bellow, a cry of rage, frustration and now satisfaction, put his head down and charged over the tryline with his teammates pushing behind him and the opponents trying to maintain a human wall in front of him. For a while the defenders seemed to have stopped him but then a second wave of leg driving took over and with another bellow Clubman popped over the line and slammed the ball down.

The game was over, the Lions had lost again but somehow the players found some joy at the end. They surrounded Clubman, slapping his back and hugging him. A brief attempt to hoist him onto shoulders was abandoned – he was simply too heavy. Xolile came trotting over from the back. "I knew you could do it," he said, squeezing the big man's shoulder.

"Thank you, thank you" he said and for a moment Xolile thought he was fighting back the tears.

"So do we have to go through this every match from now on?" Andile asked Xolile back in the change room. "A sort of Lions in-house soap opera where every emotion known to man will be on display?"

"Nah, with practice he'll be fine…"

44

Xolile sat in the toilet stall down the corridor from the team change room, his head in his hands. Where to now, he wondered. And what was he going to tell the team in the post-match talk?

The toilet stall burst open and Andile strode in. "Thought I might find you here" he said, "the guys are all a bit down. We need you to say a few words, prepare for the week of hard training ahead."

"What makes you so cheerful?" Xolile asked him grumpily.

"Ag, nothing special. You're new to the Lions, you know we lose more than we win. Come on, the season is long, we've got lots of time to recover..."

"But what happened? Why were we so shit? I can't understand what happened?"

"Two things: firstly all Super Rugby teams make lots of mistakes in the first few weeks, happens every year. Watch the highlights of all six matches this weekend you'll see we weren't alone in playing rubbish. Then for us all the talk of new beginnings, new successes, we were too tense, too anxious to do well. You'll see we'll do much better next match."

Xolile felt a sudden flash of warmth for the big man. He embraced him suddenly, briefly, almost violently (they were professional rugby players, after all) and lead him back to the change room. The atmosphere there was roughly the same as it had been in his toilet cubicle – an air of disbelief permeated the room.

"OK. That was awful – we won't play that badly again this season.

But all is not lost, it's only the first few matches. Take Sunday and Monday off and we'll meet on Tuesday morning in the seminar room at Ellis Park at 8 00 am. Then we'll plan how we'll take the Blues next week in Joburg. But before that there will be a compulsory party at Maboneng precinct on Sunday night. It's a dress up party so we want to see everyone in a costume. Right?"

45

Even Allison was concerned. "Don't all of your plans depend on the team at least being competitive?" she asked him when they met at his Japanese restaurant.

"All what plans?" he asked.

She laughed suddenly. "All those plans you have in your head that you don't tell anybody about. Isn't that true? That you have plans beyond what you've told me or the other players?"

"Maybe," said Xolile guardedly, "but you are right that if we are not even competitive then we're finished. I go, the Magnificent Seven, even Willie will be dumped in time. There are rumblings of a rebellion in the team. It seems to be gelling around arguments over who should be in the starting fifteen. If we don't start winning soon this is going to grow into a full scale insurrection. Give me the bad news from twitter."

More selected tweets:

> *Lions more mouse than king of the jungle – squeak up lads!*
>
> *My granny can tackle better than any of the Lions*
>
> *I used to love the Lions but I can't watch them anymore*
>
> *The Dagger is infected with the South African disease – petulance*

"Look at this one," said Allison. Someone called Hooker had written: *The Dagger was right – the Lions were robbed by a referee who should have been in the stands*

"Yes?" he asked somewhat puzzled.

"I wrote that," said Allison with a hint of pride.

"Oh, uh, thanks," he said. And then: "You know we don't read these mindless things for praise – just to see the temperature of the fans..."

"I'm a fan too, you know. I was just displaying my temperature."

He was silent again for a while. "Hooker, hey? Another part of the secret life of Allison perhaps?"

They chuckled away companionably.

"Or look at this one – J Louw again, remember him?"

"Oh yeah, the guy who had high hopes pre season... don't tell me he is already bitter, please don't..."

"He tweets: *so much hype same old same old I m not renewing my season ticket...*"

"Fair weather friend – isn't that what they are called? I hope Dlamini hasn't seen that one. Not renewing season tickets is something that'll get his attention."

Allison looked at him expectantly.

"What? I've got no easy answers. You know to win after three losses in a row is a hell of a lot harder than winning when you've, say, won three and lost four. The war cry and dance is coming along though. We rehearse it every day."

"Well, when is the general public going to see it? Maybe J Louw would be encouraged again."

"No we can't release it in the middle of a losing streak, after the first victory would be a good time." And then, almost shamefully: "if there is a first victory... "

46

Despite telling Allison that he had no easy answers, come Sunday evening the team had a get together, a team building exercise, Willie called it. It was a dress up party in a venue in Maboneng, chosen by Xolile.

Formerly the seamy side of the city centre, Maboneng was a few city blocks on the east side newly reclaimed as trendy young, black, creative, crime free – all those good things of the new South Africa.

They met in the bar of one of the boutique hotels. Food came in from the Ethiopian restaurant next door.

Everyone did their best to dress up – Xolile came as a geisha girl, Jeremy as Lady Gaga ("I did her in the toilet of the London Palladium two years ago" he boasted.)

Killer came as the Grim Reaper and Clubman as a small car; there were lots of Lion costumes and babies in nappies.

Willie announced: "Welcome all. We have several orders of business tonight. " A round of applause and cheers broke out. "Firstly, why are we not winning our matches? Anyone got any ideas?"

Hesitantly at first, then, like a dam wall breaking, the players produced a list of grievances. Xolile and Willie started writing down complaints but stopped after a while because they were repetitive and, as Xolile put it Allison later, frankly rubbish.

Players complained serially that:

- The captain doesn't listen to them
- The wrong team is being selected for every match

- They were overtrained
- They weren't as fit as their opponents
- The new tactics didn't work
- The old tactics were ancient and every team was doing the same
- The referees were against them
- The tactics at the breakdowns were poor
- The coach was crap

When they had finally wound down, Willie took over again.

"Firstly, to address the problem of selection of the number one team: for a change we're going to do it completely democratically. Everyone write down your starting team and reserves for Saturday. The team that takes the field will be what the majority chooses." Cheers rang out.

"Secondly something new tonight – Ethiopian food. The Dagger tells me it's like a cross between an Indian curry and West Indian type stews. After eating we'll be watching a classic film that Jeremy says moved the English team when they saw it three years ago." A few boos and ironic groans rang out.

"You dumb Saffers – it's a film about leadership and team building!" shouted Gandolfini. "Spartacus – it's a classic, directed by Stanley Kubrick."

"And then lastly, Lisa, the dance teacher, has been working with you all in small groups and more recently the whole squad. She will arrive at ten tonight and we will do five quick rehearsals of the war dance, everyone involved." More groans followed.

"But most importantly," Willie continued, "after all the effort of training and preparing for the new season…. Tonight we drink!"

Wild cheering.

The team seemed to have a very good time, all in all. Even the film was well received. "Hey, how was that part where the bosses demand to know who Spartacus is and he stands up. But before the guards can take him away someone else stands up and says 'I am Spartacus' and then another says the same and then another until all the slaves are saying they are the leader – great!" said Andile, "I can see how it worked for England."

"It didn't work" said Gandolfini, "we watched it when England were really shite…"

It was after midnight before Willie and Xolile were able to collate the results of the team's votes for the starting fifteen. They were drunk, but not as drunk as the players who were still in the room, some of whom had passed out in the corners.

"Well, well," said Willie, "I suppose this is no surprise but the majority has chosen the team I would have – all the Magnificent Seven start and the number one loose forwards and centres."

Xolile nodded. "Let's hope we can play to our potential. We need a good performance…"

"We need a bloody win!" said Willie with unaccustomed vehemence.

47

As Xolile was heading to his car he saw something out of the corner of his eye; stopped, turned, looked again, thought he was mad, then was sure. He walked over to an old GTI parked on the edge of the parking lot in the shadows where passersby could hardly see it.

Inside the car a man was banging his head against the steering wheel over and over again. What made Xolile stop was that it was one of the team....

He flung the passenger side door open and slid inside. Karel Buys, last season's flyhalf, stopped his head banging immediately and looked at Xolile in surprise. He had a red mark on his forehead; the steering wheel appeared unscathed.

"Oh, hi, Dagger," he said without any warmth.

"Karel, I don't want to intrude on a private moment but is there anything wrong? Is there anything I can do?"

"No, no, I'm fine thanks. Just... just letting off a bit of steam...."

"Well if you're sure you're OK, I'll be on my way home." Xolile put his hand on the door handle to let himself out.

"It's just that ...." said Karel hesitantly.

Xolile settled back down and Karel's story tumbled out:

"In the Sunday Times at the end of last season I was listed as the number four flyhalf in the country. So I thought, OK, I won't take the job offer at the Stormers, I'll stay with the Lions for another season at least. The oldest kid has just started primary school, my wife didn't want to leave Joburg. So I was thinking an injury or loss of form to other three ahead of me and I'll be in the World Cup squad at the end of this year. And now this, this playboy gets bought and I'm not in the Lions first choice fifteen. Poof – there goes my world cup chance. I'm 29 years old, I won't have another chance, I'll probably be too old in four years' time. So I'm screwed. If I'd taken the job offer at the Stormers at least I'd be competing for the starting spot. Now I'm a reserve permanently."

Xolile nodded in sympathy. "Yeah, I can see that things haven't worked out for you. But there are a couple of elements you haven't considered. Jeremy Gandolfini is a particular talent on attack. Come defence there is nothing he has on you but on attack he's a mystery to opponents and even to his own team. He has skills which almost no one else has – looking left and passing right or looking right and kicking to the left, very few players anywhere can do that. So what is he going to do at the Lions?

"There are only two scenarios, I think. One, he messes up – you know his weaknesses: discipline, commitment to training, women, alcohol, drugs. Anyone of these can derail his career forever. Or, two, he's a great success at the Lions and the European teams fall over themselves to buy him at prices we can't afford. Even the English national side might want him again if he does well in Super Rugby this year. So one way or another after this season he's gone. In the meantime who does he leave behind? Perhaps you – his understudy who has played a few games at flyhalf this year and several at centre, all the time watching, learning, doing at least some of the things he's so good at.

"Come 2016 you are the Lions number one flyhalf, an attacking force that no other South African team has. The three flyhalfs ahead of you

– none of them are really world beaters, you could be number one in twelve months."

Buys looked at him for a long time. "So that's all you have for me – eat it up and accept that I'm not in the starting fifteen?"

"No. I say instead of beating yourself up for a mistaken career option take this opportunity to learn, to become a more complete player, to help your team become a great one. Your glass is not half empty, it's half full. Take your chance to improve…"

They were both silent for a while. Eventually Buys said "Ok, thanks."

Xolile got out, went to his car and drove around the corner to a Kentucky Fried Chicken outlet. He ordered, paid and collected a pile of deep fried chicken. He then drove back into the parking lot.

Karl Buys was banging his head on the steering wheel again. Xolile sighed and drove home.

48

The Lions played the Blues from New Zealand at home for their next match. The Blues were regarded as contenders that year with a whole brace of young runners in their backline and a quartet of big islanders in the forwards. After three matches they were undefeated and most pundits backed the Blues to beat the Lions easily after the early season form.

The surprising part was that as the Lions left the tunnel from the change rooms the crowd, smallish, with about 15,000 people present, that is the Lions crowd, those people with Lions flags and Lions replica clothes, began to boo them.

The team was shocked, even the phlegmatic Xolile looked ashen. Andile was simply furious. "Almost ten years I've been playing at this stadium and this is the first time I've been booed by my home crowd. Who do they think they are?"

"They're the fans," answered Xolile, "if they want to boo who is to stop them? They feel it's their team letting them down."

"Well fuck them, I say. Let's bring on the war cry!"

The others nodded in agreement.

"Hang on" said Xolile "do we really want to go to war with our own fans?"

"Yes we do" said van der Merwe, the right wing.

Xolile capitulated and Andile grabbed the microphone attached to the public address system.

Allison had heard lots about the war cry but had never seen it before the match. It seemed to her to have three antecedents. Firstly, any war cry in rugby has to refer itself to the 'mother cry' – the Haka by the All Blacks. Xolile had told her they had struggled to find a cry that was at once particular to South Africa and Johannesburg but was not some higher energy version of the Haka. "We go modest the first few times we do it, although hopefully it can be pumped up for bigger matches," he had said.

The second element was implanted by the modern dance teacher Xolile had employed to give the cry and dance some grace. But the most important element was the toyi-toyi tradition of resistance to apartheid some twenty or thirty years previously. To this end the war cry was to the tune of Sobashiya Abazale which Xolile had roughly translated as follows:

We will leave our parents at home

We go in and out of foreign countries

To places our fathers and mothers don't know

Following freedom we say goodbye, goodbye, goodbye
home

We are going into foreign countries

To places our fathers and mothers don't know

Following freedom and rugby

The original Xhosa version ran as follows:

Sizobashiy' abazal' ekhaya

Saphuma sangena kwamanye 'mazwe

Lapho kungazi khon' ubaba noMam'

Silandel' inkululeko

Sithi salani, salani, salan' khaya

Sesingena kwamanye amazwe

Sizobashiya abafowethu

Saphuma sangena kwamanye 'mawze

Silandel' inkululeko norugby

The cry began with Andile, whose surprisingly fine baritone was discovered during rehearsals, signalling the start with the sound of a shell, a mortar or similar, which he made with his lips close against the microphone. The rest of the team took cover at this signal, either lying in imaginary gullies on the ground or hiding behind front row players as rocks. Then as Andile began to sing the song the others slowly emerged from hiding, initially crawling, then standing straight and finally being part of the squadron of toyi-toying dancers, marching military style towards one touchline and then the other.

The dance trainer had played them an excerpt from the slave chorus of Beethoven's Fidelio which featured the prisoner slaves being released from several years in the dungeons. They slowly straighten up as they sing the famous chorus 'Der Freier Luft' – the free air, a celebration of freedom. The Lions had borrowed generously from it.

"This is Joburg," said Andile, "the chance of more than one in a thousand being familiar with an opera is remote."

The war cry is a short one, just over a minute usually, and ends with the song being bellowed by the players and the dancing ending in a pyramid with the smallest player, in this case Snake, being hoisted aloft as he points at the sky with a clenched fist.

The crowd was silent when the Lions finished the war cry with a somewhat puzzled scattered hand clap breaking out here and there.

"I feel great!" said Andile to the team, "Now we slaughter them..."

49

The Blues kicked off deep and Xolile took the ball confidently on the 22. He kicked it back and in turn the Blues flyhalf, number three officially in the New Zealand national flyhalf stakes, kicked it into touch on the half way line.

There was a bit of too and fro before the line out formed. Allison and the girls were seated in a box, "I still hate rugby" said Leah, "but these seats are cool."

"Should be" said Allison, "they're the best seats in the stadium." They sat in a corporate box, arranged by Xolile. They reclined in comfy seats with sausage rolls on plates in front of them. Allison sipped her brandy and coke and looked over at the TV screen above her.

The commentator was saying: 'Here we are at the first line out and already something strange is going on. In fact, Blades, I've never seen anything like this: the first line out to the Lions is being thrown by a lock. The hooker, Andile Phike, is in the front – I suppose it's a short throw and a drive by the hooker, don't you think?'

'I think that's it exactly; not sure how this is going to surprise the Blues. Of course, the Lions are fielding a couple of players with virtually no rugby experience. Could it be that this lock, the one they call Clubman, doesn't know where he is supposed to stand in the line out?'

Allison watched as Clubman hurled the ball, with an odd wind up by rugby standards, into the void. The ball soared up, up, up – it seemed to hang in the air for ages…

"Surely that's not in straight!" she could hear the commentator bleat in the background. Eventually the ball headed towards the ground, a good 30 metres past the lineout, now effectively in no man's land between the two defensive lines.

And from almost nowhere, with what seemed like acres of space and time at his disposal, Xolile ran on to the ball, gathered it just before it touched the ground, and headed for the corner. The Blues defence reacted immediately with both centre and wing on the left converging on him, pushing him towards the touchline. And then, again almost in slow motion, all three players went over the touchline. They looked up and saw Jim Mahlangu dotting down the ball underneath the posts. The ref called for a video replay, querying a forward pass. They had to show the segment three times before Allison, and the video ref, could see the little flip pass under Xolile's body to Jim as he crashed over the touch line.

As the try was acknowledged by the ref, Jeremy Gandolfini drop kicked the conversion and the Lions congregated on the half way line where an impassioned Xolile addressed them.

"Nice start for once," he told them, "never mind what I say now, it's just to make the opposition think we've got a whole agenda up our sleeves." He then slipped into Xhosa, which only a handful of his teammates understood, and delivered a Churchillian type tirade complete with shouts, finger pointing and lots of fists slapping into palms.

Andile told Allison later that Xolile had delivered a page from the Xhosa bible about Jesus riding a donkey into town. "I had to hold myself to stop laughing" he told her, "I kept on imagining a naughty young Xolile having to learn that passage off by heart after coming late to Sunday school."

The crowd was buzzing – so many things seemed to have happened in the first ten minutes. The Blues came back like the great team they were – a series of phased plays and clever back line darts and feints brought them two kickable penalties in the next ten minutes – 7 to 6 to the Lions.

At the twenty minute mark the Lions got a penalty inside their own twenty two. Gandolfini got touch near the halfway line and Xolile marched up and down the lineout, calling 'chicken wings, chicken wings'. The ball was thrown in, the Lions took it, mauled it up briefly and then set about the chicken wing manoeuvre.

The chicken wing, as Allison explained to her daughters, was an idea that originated with Jeremy Gandolfini. In its simplest form it was an inversion of the customary division between forwards and backs in a running, attacking format. The forwards cluster in two groups of four about ten metres from either touchline, while the backs spread across the centre of the field. The ball would be passed from back to deep lying back from one side of the field to the other. In this process, the attacking backs would probe for weaknesses in their opponents – a defender who came out of the line to make a potential space to attack or one who was slower than his mates to come up in a line, there were several possibilities, she told Leah.

But the critical thing was that no contact was sought by the backline unless there was a clear advantage to be had. Once the ball got to one pod of forwards on one side or the other then contact would be made, ideally against a group of backs or a smaller number of forwards. The attacking forwards would attempt to maul it up and cross the advantage line. Whether they achieved this or not, maintaining possession was critical. The forward drive would end when the half backs started the swing across the centre of the field with the backs again.

Xolile had said they were not worried about going backwards – when they practised it the team generally lost about ten metres with the backline part of the manoeuvre but made it up again when the forwards drove forward. "But we can't let it go for too long otherwise the opposition forwards will begin to set up on the wings as well," he had said.

Allison counted four sweeps across the field. So far the Blues defence had been puzzled but resolute and no gaps had been created. On the fifth sweep Xolile feinted right inside Gandolfini although the passage of the movement was to the left. The opposing flyhalf and centre shuffled involuntarily to the right – Xolile was the finisher after all – and Gandolfini passed left to Jim Mahlangu who had come up between the centres.

Jim came out of the Lions line like a cannon ball. He bounced off the Blues outside centre and headed for the corner flag. There was plenty of cover defence around because of the unstructured set up by the Lions so he had lots to do. Xolile followed him and kept within five metres of his flying form. Xolile held his hands out and signalled to be given the ball while he screamed at him in Zulu to 'go go go'. Some defenders still held off expecting the ball to be slipped back to Xolile but Jim had no such plans. He went off to the left at his full, breathtaking pace, slipping past the grasping hands of the full back, he crashed through a tackle by the covering eighth man and then scored the try with both Blues flanks holding on to his lower body.

Xolile and he had spent much time discussing the dive for the TV cameras when one scored ("We'll be scoring lots of tries" Xolile had told him confidently.)

Xolile wanted to keep his low key dot-em-down approach and by contrast Jim was going for the classic dive with the ball in outstretched hands, no smashing the ball into the ground as was popular with big wings.

And this he did with his second try of the evening. "That's got to be one of the season's most spectacular tries" said the commentator on TV as the crowd finally found its voice.

"Who is this kid?" he asked. The crowd went wild – to a man they stood and cheered and screamed and applauded as Jim walked back to his position.

Xolile went up to him. "See? This is what it feels like... Better than winning a race isn't it?"

"It's better than sex even" answered Jim.

"You knew about this Chicken wing thing? Is that what you and wonder boy spend all those hours talking about?" Leah asked Allison.

"Well... yes. There are five new tactics the Lions have been practising. So far we've seen two of them – the chicken wing and the javelin. If the other three come up I'll try and point them out."

The Lions entered the second half with a ten point cushion. Willie had warned them in the change room to expect the Blues to come 'hard' at them.

"We need to move immediately to the Sandton station part of the moustache manoeuvre," he told them.

From the kick off at the start of the second half the Lions went in to slow tempo phase. The spectators probably did not realise what was planned at first. Only Allison, primed by Xolile as to the nature of the tactic, saw it immediately.

"Watch" she told her daughters and one or two hangers on in the box who seemed to gravitate to her as an authority, "this is the Sandton variation – it's aimed to slow the game down just as the opponents want to speed it up..."

As she spoke, a scrum was reset for the second time.

"Why would the Lions want to do that?" asked Leah, "surely you can't win the game that way?"

"Well you can win eventually; but look at it from the Blues side: their coach has just told them to get the ball and run at the Lions. They have a star studded backline all of whom could be international stars if they played anywhere else but in New Zealand. So they come out fired up for the start of the second half – and that happens..."

As she spoke a pushing and shoving dispute broke out between Killer and his opposing tight head prop. Other Lions came in to the dispute, more pushing and shoving ensued, other players came running in and it took a minute or two for the ref to restore order. Then the referee asked for time off and a replay to see if there was any foul play.

"But time is off now," said Leah, "how does that help waste time?"

"It's still disruptive to the Blues' rhythm. The Lions are not playing for the end of the match, there's still 35 minutes to go, but playing to nullify their opponents before attacking again."

Now there was a line out to the Lions near the half way line. Andile seemed to be struggling to hear the lineout call from Clubman. He made his way back to the giant lock three times with his hand theatrically behind his ear.

"Isn't this bad sportsmanship?" asked Rosemary, "Shouldn't the teams be trying to beat each other fair and square?"

"You could argue that it is stretching the bounds of fair play. I think in sport it's called 'gamesmanship' – something that's on the borderline of unfair..."

As Allison spoke the Blues' frustration boiled over into a silly penalty for not releasing the player on the ground. Gandolfini stroked the ball over from just inside the half way line. The Lions now lead by 13.

"And then why's it called 'the Sandton variation'?" Rosemary again.

"I don't understand this perfectly but it seems to be the motif of a railway station. Park Station, which is busy working class station in Central Johannesburg for when the game is to be played at highest tempo. And then Sandton Station which is a measured, middle class, not very crowded station for when the team needs to play slow tempo, like now. Why this is called the moustache manoeuvre overall, I've no idea."

Five minutes later, the Blues conceded another penalty, Gandolfini kicked for a lineout five metres from the try line and the Lions forwards mauled it over for their third try. With a twenty point lead, the game was effectively over as a contest and the Sandton was called off.

With 20 minutes to go and with the Lions 15 points up and in search of a bonus point fourth try, Xolile called "Park Station moustache!" as the replacements came on.

With the Lions playing high tempo rugby and the Blues responding in kind the last quarter of the game was a fan's delight – four great tries were scored, two to the Lions and two to the Blues.

Jim completed his hat trick with a try on full time in a deliciously graceful one two with Xolile where each handled the ball twice before the final pass sent him away for a spectacular dive to crown the afternoon.

At the final whistle, booing was a distant memory to the crowd as they rose as one to salute a fine performance by the home team.

50

"Dagger, that must be a relief for you and the team, to finally register a win this season?"

"Huge relief. Particularly against the Blues, who are a great team and should be contenders for the title. We might even meet them again later in the season during the playoffs."

"And lots of new tactics on display from your team. Is this part of your new approach? And are there others we haven't seen yet?"

"You know, we believe that in the modern game one can't simply play phases. Depending on the opposition a good team has to have a whole range of set moves and occasional tactics to surprise their opponents. We've got hundreds more that we plan to use later in the year..."

"And this new guy Mahlangu, three tries today, he really looked like something special. He has the reputation of being the fastest man to have played rugby anywhere, anytime – do you think that's true?"

"I really couldn't say. He clearly is dangerously fast – and imagine how good he's going to be once we teach him the rules."

"And the new war cry? Took everybody by surprise, I think. Unusual to direct it against your supporters, what is the origin of this war dance?"

"Well I'm not sure war cry is the right word for it. It's rooted in South Africa's particular history where protesters, usually kids, defied the full might of a military regime to pursue freedom and social justice. The toyi toyi we used today is not so much a dance for war as a 'come and join us' appeal, more whimsical song than one would expect challenging a ruthless state..."

"And it's going to be a feature of all your future games?"

"Definitely."

"Dagger, always interesting chatting to you; good luck for the rest of the season."

51

"We've done and congratulations. Let's keep the drinking in proportion tonight – remember the various disasters after we won against the Crusaders last season, yes?"

Several players nodded in agreement. For most the post match elation had worn off with the obligatory ice baths. Joy and fatigue seemed to go hand in hand and so for once Willie's warnings did not seem to fall on deaf ears. As they filed out, Jim asked to speak to Xolile.

"Uh, Boss?"

"What, Jim?"

"I don't really like it when you tell the press that I can't play, don't know the rules, you're going to teach me the game when you have the time. It's a bit insulting to me, I think..."

Xolile nodded gravely as if considering the matter. "But you do know the rules and how to play – everyone in the team realises that. So it's just what I say that you object to." Jim nodded.

"Look, Jim, more than any of us, you have a huge future in front of you. You'll be likely to play many, many games for the Springboks, you'll probably retire a wealthy man from playing in Europe. So if I tell the other teams this season that you are green, a newbie, a naïf, what do they think? They say to themselves this guy's a runner, sure, but he can't tackle, he can't field a kick or pass or maintain his line in defence. While they think that, for those few weeks or months till they realise you are a more complete player, it's to our team's advantage. So why would you object to that?"

Jim was silent for a while. "Few weeks or months only?" he asked eventually.

Xolile nodded.

"A naïf, you just called me. Is that like a primitive? A native?"

"Yes, I suppose these are all the same terms, more or less..."

Jim rose to leave. "Are you sure you're a black man?" he tossed over his shoulder.

Xolile's laughter boomed out at his departing back.

52

In August, the rugby world was rocked by a fresh scandal. Andrew Macdonald, the Scottish captain, was drug tested and found to have traces of cocaine, heroin and ecstasy in his blood. After a lengthy debate in the English press Macdonald was banned from all rugby for twelve months.

Xolile tweeted: *Don't know this Macdonald guy but he seems to have had a raw deal – since when are heroin and ecstasy performance enhancing drugs in rugby?*

This produced a predictable storm of response. The South African War on Drugs committee called immediately for an apology from Xolile. "For someone of his experience to defend the consumption of addictive, personality-altering illegal drugs is reprehensible. International rugby players are often role models for young people. To advocate taking drugs is completely irresponsible of Mr Dalindyebo."

Xolile tweeted back: *Why is it that rugby players are always the bad guys? Does Tiger Woods get tested for heroin before each tournament? Does Roger Federer or Serena Williams?*

And then later: *if I am a role model for anyone, unlikely I know, it's because I play rugby not because of what I do in my off times*

More twitter fencing followed. Xolile lost interest in the topic but Allison found the issue fascinating. Writing as the hooker she referred tweeters to a link to a supplement by the Economist, the respected British business magazine. The Economist opposed the American sponsored war on drugs for several reasons: it hadn't worked (drug usage across the world was higher than ever before); it had destabilized countries who were primary drug producers (like Mexico, Columbia, Afghanistan and others); it had created in the USA and other countries an entire prison population of users and dealers, often where the victims of their crimes were hard to indentify.

In its stead, The Economist proposed that drugs should be legalized and sold freely by multinational drug companies. Any individual would be free to buy what they liked, just as they could do with alcohol.

Allison defended their position spiritedly online, holding four or five debates simultaneously before the topic died a natural death.

53

Allison phoned Xolile at the end of practice. "Check out Newscloud on your smart phone and I'll call you back in five," she said.

When she called back Xolile had found the news item. "Who is it? Do you know?" he asked her.

"I don't... but I may be able to find out. If I can, should I sms the name to you?"

"Yeah..." He was a bit abstracted. "No, don't tell me till I ask you for it. I think it better if I raise it with the team while I don't know who it is. Join us at 5 if you can, we might need to manage this from a journalist point of view."

The viewing room was full, all 30 players and ten coaches and ancillary staff present when Allison arrived. She had failed to uncover the name of the player but when she whispered as such to Xolile he seemed unconcerned. He got to his feet and called for attention.

"You all know my assistant, Allison, right? I've asked her to join us for reasons that will become apparent in a while. I'll get straight to the point," Xolile began, "Newscloud today reported on a divorce proceeding instituted by a certain Charmaine Wiese. She alleges that her husband, a man of considerable wealth otherwise she wouldn't bother, had been having an affair with a member of the Lions squad..."

He didn't get any further before he was interrupted by a cascade of comment and laughter. He didn't call for order but let the noise mount and run like a cloud of steam.

Allison noted that the first response was denial – 'Ah, bullshit, man' was a common one. Then there was the bravado: 'It's you, I know it's you'.

And then finally the machismo: 'We won't have moffies, not in my team'.

Eventually Xolile called for order. "Remember what we said before: players' personal things are important to the team only as far as they affect the team. So when the press ask us tomorrow how we feel about having gay players in the squad we say what exactly – that there are none and if there were, we wouldn't play with them? Is that our position?"

More debate followed but more structured now. Several players expressed concern about the intimacy of scrumming with gay men and what to do if a gay man came on to them.

Suddenly Gandolfini's voice rose above the rest: "I did a bloke when I was at University. About three or four times, then we stopped cos I started dating that model. Wasn't bad, but I prefer women, for sure, yeah?"

The room was silent. Even Xolile stared at Gandolfini, mouth open in a parody of surprise. What a strange lad, thought Allison, he's got such a huge ego he is almost ego free – it didn't occur to him for a moment that his teammates might judge him for his last revelation.

Then another voice rang out, this time from Sarel Prinsloo, the outside centre: "I am gay!" he said in a firm tone.

More silence – then Andile sprang to his feet. "No, I'm gay" he yelled. Then a moment later Xolile did the same – "I'm gay" he shouted. Then the room was filled with hundred kilogram rugby players shouting 'I'm gay!'

Players were laughing so hard that several had tears in their eyes. Allison, who had never seen Kubrick's film Spartacus, nor the scene they referred to where the identity of the leader was protected by mass volunteering, was completely befuddled by the turn of events. Who can understand these men, she thought to herself, animals one minute, little boys the next...

Prinsloo was not to be denied. When the laughter had died down to just chuckles he continued "I've always been gay, since I was little, and I've played rugby professionally for five years, laughing at gay jokes, making sexist remarks about women. I'm done with that from today – I'm done with lying and pretending. If you want to kick me out of the team then go ahead. But I'm not the guy in the divorce case – I've never met these people."

"Wait a minute," said Willie, "you mean we've got two gay players in the squad?"

"I'm the one in the newspapers," said Killer quietly from the back of the room.

54

More shock followed. In the silence that ensued, Killer continued in his matter of fact voice that commanded attention.

"I'm sorry if my habits have placed the team in a difficult position. Like Prinsloo here I've been hiding my true nature from everyone, friends, family, team members. The affair with Gideon Wiese ended two years ago but is now coming to court. Some of you might wonder why I have so many issues – first the killing and now the gayness. In fact they are the same issue. The cops saw me the previous night coming out of a gay club in Pretoria. They wanted to shake me down or they said they would expose me to the press. That's when things started getting physical between us. My therapist says that my rage is a product of my not being real about my sexual identity..."

"You've got a therapist?" exclaimed Andile.

Killer continued in an unruffled manner. "She says that if I am to heal and move on from the death I need to come out...."

Now he paused. "This is me coming out. And I will abide by the judgement of the team. But I just want to add this, although it is a bit difficult for me to say this in public: I am generally attracted to small men, not big ones like in this room. From a sexual point of view none of you are my sexual types."

"Not even the Dagger?" shouted Gandolfini.

Discussion ebbed and flowed for a while. To Allison it seemed that other players were saying that they couldn't afford to lose the Killer but could lose Prinsloo.

Eventually Xolile recognised Jason who had had his hand up in a schoolboy fashion for some time.

"Go, Snake" he cued him.

Jason began speaking, trying to make his accent understandable. "What is it that makes this Lions team great? What makes the team special? It's because we take people that no one else wants, the players that are forgotten or cast aside for one reason or another. Whether it's drugs or fighting or black players no one wants – this is their home, this Lions team. So if some of us want to have sex with men it's none of our business but they are still our team, our comrades. Because we're a team."

Scattered applause broke out.

"So Snake, let me get this right," Xolile went on, "if the press asks about gay players in the Lions team we say what?"

"We say *hulle is onse…* they are ours!" replied Jason.

General agreement seemed to be evident now to Allison.

"You know we've talked about disarming the crowds in foreign venues – this might help," put in Willie, "the fact that we're a gay friendly team, if I can use that term, this could be a factor in getting support at places like Sydney, or Cape Town or Durban."

"I agree" said Xolile, "but let's make absolutely sure that everyone is on the same page. Are we all ok to have gay players in the team?"

"Yes!"

"No exception?"

"No!"

"And over time our gay members will guide us on what words they find offensive – no more talk of moffies or poofdahs, right? Then Allison I'd like you to work with Killer and Prinsloo to erect a gay supporter's website so we can explore Willie's idea of getting more support. And you can interview me about gay players."

55

The Star March 18ᵗʰ

Allison Meyer interviews Xolile Dalindyebo

AM: Xolile, you take on the Reds this Saturday at Ellis Park. Fresh from a great victory over the Blues, what's the mood in the team?

XD: We are very upbeat at the moment. It's great to see some of the areas we've been working on, like the scrums and lineouts, the breakdowns, improving steadily. Plus we scored a number of good tries against the Blues so we should take this good form into the next game.

AM: And the injury situation?

XD: Chimmy has a dead leg but we expect him to be fully recovered by Saturday. For the rest bumps and bruises, nothing major.

AM: What about the war cry? What are the roots of this song and dance?

XD: The roots of the song are quite extensive. It was first sung to the tune of a hymn in the old Transkei when young men would go off to work in the gold mines of Johannesburg. It was a song that celebrated home but also asked for support in this journey because many mineworkers never came back, either dying of TB or underground or else settling in the mining towns, becoming urbanized. The second life for the song was as a farewell when guerrillas left to fight the border war against the then fascist government. Once again, many were not to return. We use it similarly as we go off to battle on the rugby fields in New Zealand and Australia. The dancing part we made up ourselves mostly from the toyi-toyi, the insurrectionary dance of the kids in the 90's – plus we had some advice from professional choreographers.

AM: Some people say the revolutionary roots of the song are sacred and you've trivialized it, almost, by using it for rugby.

XD: We could debate this, of course, but we don't see how any song can be sacred. The question really is whether it has any meaning for today, not where it comes from. And that we'll only be sure of, one way or the other, with the passage of time.

AM: And any comment on Cecil Oliphant's being named as a gay partner in a divorce case.

XD: Obviously we support Killer fully in this time of stress and media attention. I understand this is an old relationship which no longer is current for any of the parties involved. We're encouraging Killer to focus on the game on Saturday and put all this media hype behind him.

AM: And you knew he was gay?

XD: Of course. We have no secrets within the team – and in fact we have several gay players in our group and this is known to everyone in the team without it being the subject of the back page of the Sunday papers. The world is full of gay rugby players and fans – it's a complete non-issue for the Lions.

AM: Tell us about the Javelin throw, how it came about and under what circumstances you will use it again.

XD: Well, Allison, it's very simple…

56

Tuesday evening and Xolile treated Allison and Andile to his new past time – a Chinese man who could do Japanese style massages.

The three of them lay face down on massage tables.

"Give us the latest social news on the Lions, Allison, we just work there, we're always the last to know what's happening…."

"The most comment is in fact on the War Cry." Allison's voice came from a recess in the massage table, giving her a slight boom and echo in the small room.

"The Military Veterans Group has criticised it as trivialising the struggle…"

"What nonsense!" burst out Andile.

"While the Veterans Military Group, I might have these names wrong, this is from memory, say that this is a way of passing on our history to the next generation."

"Perfect response for us," said Xolile, "what about the rugby?"

"Mitchell Coutts, probably the most respected rugby journalist in the country…"

"Besides Allison Meyer" put in Andile loyally.

"Said he was astonished at how many novel tactics the Lions showed up with on Saturday. He said that if this is the standard of the play going forward then you could well be in with a chance for a playoff position. Most of the other journalists put much store in Jim's performance, calling him raw but perhaps a Springbok in the making. Coutts, however, singled out Gandolfini for a man of the match performance."

"I agree" said Andile, "he was completely in charge on Saturday."

"Your breakdown consultant, Jake Rawlinson, arrives from the University of Wellington tomorrow. He should be at the Gautrain station around 2 pm. Who's going to meet him?"

"Andile, you stay at training, Allison and I will fetch him, settle him at the hotel and then hopefully he starts work next week. I suppose he needs to watch a game before he can coach?"

"Then he travels with the team to Australasia after we play the Reds on Saturday, so it's just a hello for ten days in Joburg, right?" Andile grunted as the masseur found a spasmed muscle bundle in his massive shoulders.

"That's the plan but breakdowns are so important that if he can make a difference we'll keep him for the whole season. On email he said that a month of teaching and reflecting would be all he has to give. Allison, how's the desensitization of the gay boys going?"

"Pretty well. We went through every known insult for gay people in this country. You know I read somewhere that Icelanders have fifty words for snow – in this country we have more than fifty expressions for gay men. About ten of them have the word 'fudge' in them…"

"Keep at it. I want them to laugh at their opponents when they call them names – and practice is the only way to achieve that. Within a week or three all this gay stuff will die down and they can get back to normal work."

Gcobani Bobo and Elvis Jack

57

Xolile and Allison sat on a bench near the exit of the Sandton Gautrain station.

"That's him, surely," said Allison. They watched as a fit young man with a backpack and sweat stained cap with a New Zealand flag on it strode towards them.

"Jakes?' said Xolile as he rose.

"Nope, sorry, my name is Arthur" said the visitor with a smile.

They sat back down again.

"You've got plans for the overseas tour?" Allison asked.

"Only the most basic. We play the Highlanders and Chiefs first in New Zealand and if we can win those two Willie is suggesting we should field the second team against the Waratahs in Sydney, then hopefully come back to a full side and full points against the Western Force in Perth. We'll be staying in that block of flats you persuaded Dlamini to buy in Hamilton and this'll be our base for the whole tour."

"I saw that in the whole history of Super Rugby no South African team has got more than 13 points out of the four overseas games..."

"We need more than that ideally but right now ..."

"Dagger?"

They looked round. A small woman in her late twenties with a tight short sleeved t shirt and muscular arms stood next to them with a rucksack on her hip.

"... Jakes?" said Xolile.

58

Jakes stood at the lectern in front of the whole team. When she spoke in public, Xolile noticed, she slowed her speech down and was much more understandable than when she spoke New Zealand, guttural, often with no verbs, in a conversation.

"So when the Dagger met me yesterday it was like going on a blind date – he was thinking: how did I link up with this dog, in a breakdown sense." General laughter around the room.

"So this is me: I don't like talking about meself much but in a nutshell I come from a rugby mad family. I played two games for the Black Ferns, the All Black women's team for those who don't know, till I did me knee in, in 2010. I have a Masters in Breakdown Theory from the University of Auckland and I currently am the breakdown coach for Manawatu, that's a New Zealand provincial side. I'm not gay but I don't date rugby players – it's like taking my work home for me." More laughter.

"While I was in the plane I looked at your last three matches on video. Then when I arrived I noticed that the Dagger met me and not someone from the management side. This leads to me two conclusions. One, you're a great side with loads of talent and new ideas but your breakdowns are, well, shit, there's no other word for it. Secondly, seeing that my salary is coming from Allison I assume the Dagger is paying and he's not pleased at having hired a woman. So I have to show the value of my skills to the team if I am to remain here past the first month. Make sense?"

General nods.

"With my size and strength I can't behave like a usual coach. I can't get down with you, I'm too small. But these are my tools – my laptop and my projector. And in these tools I can show you how to respond better to breakdown situations. I also am working on some linked modules – the counter ruck, and ball presentation in the tackle – but breakdowns are where it's at for me. From your videos it was obvious that you didn't know what you were doing at the breakdown, got penalised heavily in the first few matches and responded by holding off, by surrendering the breakdown in your last two matches – unnecessary."

She paused, looked round the room. "Can I go on?" More nods and murmurs.

"At the first breakdown penalty you'll know what referee you are dealing with. There are only four types in my world – Northern Hemisphere style, Southern Hemisphere style, hybrids, and know-nothings. Once you have put the referee in the right box you proceed by asking yourself three questions in each situation – except when dealing with a know nothing ref, then you have only two questions. Now I'm going to go through each ref type and each question in some detail..."

Half an hour later Andile smsed Xolile "I'm in love; can we keep her?"

59

The Lions took on the Reds on a lovely Highveld winter afternoon. The air was chill but the sun was out and it was warm out of the shade. More than 40,000 good humoured fans turned out. Was the crowd blacker than usual? Hard to be sure, Xolile and Andile agreed.

"They should make the fans fill out a racial block when they buy tickets," said Andile.

The Lions under 21 side were roped in to instruct the crowd on the war cry, block by block. When the Lions took the field the words were put up on the big screen and a good few of the crowd sang along.

But in a joyful afternoon for the locals, rugby was the big winner. Temporarily freed from hiding in the closet both Killer and the centre Sarel Prinsloo had big games. The Lions scrum was dominant and suddenly it wasn't just from the tight head side as the Killer chomped up his opposite number.

Breakdowns were improved – only four penalties conceded versus five turnovers. "Better," said Jakes laconically to Andile after the game.

And in the backline Jeremy taunted the Reds by threatening repeatedly to unleash Xolile or Jim. Consequently gaps opened in the centre and Sarel went through them like an express train. At the end of the game, another six try romp for the home side, the Lions had five points on the log before they took to the overseas leg of their campaign. But best of all, said Willie, we did it without going back to the javelin or chicken leg tactics.

"If the teams in Australasia look only at our last game we can still surprise them with those techniques. By the way we have a mini front row crisis – only four fit front rankers available. I'm taking your fat boy from Welkom on tour, just in case," he told Xolile.

"Tsego? Let's hope we won't need him," said Andile.

"And even more," Xolile told Allison the night before they left for New Zealand, "sometime on the overseas trip we're going to unveil the 'fourteen' – and that might make the rugby world sit up...."

60

The squad settled into the new digs, a three storey student residence just off the centre of Hamilton. That evening Willie addressed everyone from a list issues on a typed sheet of paper.

"This list comes from Allison – is there anything that woman can't do? Firstly, the aim is to settle in to your rooms for the duration of the Australasian tour. If we make the playoffs in Aus or New Zealand we'll come back here.

"There's a list of five pubs within walking distance of here – remember this is not home, you can't drink and drive in this country. We expect everyone to make regular appearances at the pubs, even if you don't drink. And if your English is poor or you're a bit shy, don't worry – the locals will be happy to strike up conversations with you. If you should want to bring a friend home the three rooms on the top floor are permanently vacant – just lock the door behind you, clean up after you and leave the room open when you're... uh... done.

"There's a disabled children's home on the other side of town. Allison has made contact with the matron. She wants us to meet the kids as usual but she also wants a wall built on the one side of the school. Neil Gouws is in charge of that, those who want to help please speak to him afterwards. The materials we'll buy locally from the Dagger's fund."

"If there's a need to save a rhino please let me know," put in Gandolfini.

Willie chose to take him literally: "Yeah, Jeremy, and what will you do about it?"

"I'll stick his horns on the front of my car."

"Then the usual warning: for many kids the thrill of meeting a professional rugby player is about provoking him to violence. The locals cannot lose in this game – if they beat you in a fight the newspapers and their friends will go to town; if you beat them it's because you're bigger and do this kind of thing for a living. So you fight with locals, no matter what the circumstances, no matter what the provocation, you can't win and the locals can't lose. Clear?"

"So what do we do if someone looks for shit with us?" a voice from the back called.

"You do the smart thing – walk away. If you can't do that then phone me or the Dagger and we'll come and fetch you, no matter what the time.

"There are three schools in the area, we've got permission to train at two of them so far. If the school kids hang about be nice to them. We'll probably have at least one teaching session at each, maybe show them the chicken wing or the 14 or something…"

"Oh yes," said Spickles, "so that they can learn it and beat us in three years' time when they play senior rugby."

"And lastly," Willie went on, "remembering what went down with Andile last year, my advice is no sex on the first date and ask to see the birth certificate on the second date."

General laughter as the team filed out, heading for the pubs.

61

The day dawned for the game against the Highlanders with New Zealand putting on its best winter face – that is the sun was shining weakly, the wind was only a few notches below gale force and the temperature was simply biting. The Highlanders had their own problems this season so far with four losses out of seven and a growing injury list of regular players.

The Lions did their war dance, accompanied mostly by derision from the smallish crowd. A small group of fans clustered behind a banner reading 'Otago gay and lesbian coalition for the Lions'. Allison caught them late in the match cheering for the Highlanders as a reflex.

The Lions played with great confidence and authority. They were in charge at scrum time as usual, used the Dagger and Jim to torment their opponents down the left flank, and in a Park station moustache manoeuvre just before half time scored two spectacular tries, with Jason for once being on the final pass for his first try of the season.

In the second half the Lions began to turn ball over regularly at the breakdown. The javelin was tried twice but failed to make an impression. Jim and Xolile, however, capped a ten minute period of the chicken wing with a try each.

The game was already over as a contest, five minutes to play when a scrum went down near the halfway line. As the players disengaged, with the usual pushing and shoving by the front rows, the Highlanders tight head prop was heard clearly on the ref's microphone saying to Killer: "Are all the front rankers faggots or is it just you?"

The question was heard clearly by the millions of TV watchers but the spectators at the stadium were not privy to the ref's microphone – and nor were any of the players further than five metres from the scrum area. So when the ref held up a yellow card for the tight head and announced "bigoted remark" many people at the stadium were completely bewildered. If the Highlanders had been closer in score the crowd's response might well have been more vigorous than low key booing as the prop trudged off the field.

Bonus point victory and job done.

Jakes burst in to the change room just as the first beers were distributed.

"Hey," said Jim, "naked men here…"

"Don't give a shit," said Jakes, "Great work at the breakdown, really great, 100 per cent better than any other game I've seen you play."

The female interviewer after the match was buoyant.

"Dagger, what we just saw was the first time a player was disciplined for gender preference remarks – perhaps a sign that all sport will follow. You pleased?"

"Not at all. I thought it was a bad decision and I hope never to see it repeated."

"You mean because rugby players will be more sensitive in future?"

Xolile cocked his head to one side as though he were speaking to someone who was slightly retarded. "No I mean it was a bad decision because a player was disciplined for a variant of swearing. Anyone who has ever played competitive rugby knows that when an opponent hurts you – and that happens many times per game at this level – one of the techniques, one of the safety valves that stops one player from hitting another is to swear at them. Everybody does it and it seems pointless to try and outlaw it."

"Do the newly outed gay players in the Lions feel the same way? Aren't they pleased about the referee's protection?"

"I haven't checked with them, I'm giving you my opinion. I don't think any of us need the ref's protection, though, at least not from words – we can look after ourselves, whether we are gay or not."

The interviewer stood her ground: "But surely, Dagger, you are conflating swearing and bigotry? They are not the same thing..."

"But how far apart are they? Let me give you an example: one of the commonest insults in all contact sports, cricket, rugby, soccer, basketball, is for someone to make a reference to having had sex with another player's loved one. This can be a wife, girlfriend, sister, mother or even a grandmother. This is done to upset the other player to such an extent that he cannot think straight and becomes a lesser player.

"So to extend the gay motif let's say I say to Ben Opiolotto I had sex with your father last night and he loved it, he begged me for more. It's a crude and shocking thing and that's why it gets said. He replies: you dog, you faggot, I'll kill you. Now according to you he would get sent off and I wouldn't. Does this make sense to anyone?"

In the next forty eight hours the five minute excerpt on the internet went viral with over 300,000 hits. Thousands of comments were appended.

It even spawned an international club: *#sticksnstones* was formed initially in Melbourne with the avowed aim of decriminalising all words. Their slogan was 'Words don't hurt; sticks and stones do.'

Membership was limited but opponents to the movement, some of them organised into *"#Wordscanhurt"*, were vociferous on all social media platforms.

A Sydney journalist offered Xolile 100,000 Aus dollars to do an extended interview on this topic. He declinded politely.

Andile Whatsaped Allison: "You know sometimes I wish the Dagger would just shut up."

62

The next game, against the Chiefs in Waikato stadium, was billed by journalists as one of the match ups of the year. The Chiefs were a huge favourite with local fans and had big men, most of them from the south sea islands of Fiji and Samoa, at both forward and back.

Allison had just turned 38 and combined the occasion with watching the game on TV. She served sushi to her twenty odd guests and family members.

"Xolile teach you to make sushi?" asked brother in law Mitch.

"No, I bought a book; this probably wouldn't be of good enough quality for him."

They all settled in front of the new big screen TV. "What's new from the team?" asked Mike.

"According to Xolile on Skype, a few bumps and bruises only. They are waiting to unleash the '14' manoeuvre, maybe do it today."

The game was unrelenting. For once the Lions had no advantage at the scrums with the collisions being keenly contested and often resulting in collapses and the inevitable penalties.

The two teams played a similar style – no kicking, smashing the ball up to make repeated rucks and every now and then a volley of sleight of hand passing to try and breach the opposition defence. The truth was, said Allison, that the Chiefs seemed to be doing it better than the Lions. At half time the Lions were three points behind and it appeared to be anybody's match.

About fifteen minutes in to the second half, the Lions lost the ball on attack and the Chiefs centre broke away on the half way line on the right hand side of the field. Xolile had been up on the attacking manoeuvre and there was simply no one between the centre and the Lions' goal line.

"Well, that's all over, Red Rover," said the New Zealand commentator.

"No wait that Malangoo – no, he can never catch him..." The second commentator was referring to Jim (Malangoo was as close as he could come to his surname) who was pelting from the left wing to try and catch the Chiefs centre. Jim was a good twenty metres behind him with only fifty or so metres to the Lions try line.

"Like heck, he can catch him, but can he bring him down?" The crowd watched in silence as the fastest man in world rugby hauled in the Chiefs centre, metre by metre. Afterwards, in the replays, Mitch observed that Jim was effectively running twice as fast as one of the best backs in New Zealand rugby.

"Oh oh oh!"

Five metres from the tryline and Jim pulled him down with a classic tackle from behind, round his knees. The centre tried to roll over but by then Xolile had arrived and the two of them forced a penalty for not releasing.

Play was briefly interrupted as every member of the Lions team rushed up to embrace Jim. Solo tries usually had a less enthusiastic series of congratulations.

"Mum, what's going on?" asked Rosemary, "I mean that was good, great even, I can see that, but why are the other players making such a fuss?"

"Because a few months ago Jim had never tackled anyone in his life – and he's put in hundreds of hours, taken hundreds of hits and missed tackles just for this one moment, this one moment of greatness to save his team seven points..."

The Lions and Chiefs swopped tries and penalties for the next twenty minutes. But when the final twenty minutes of the match dawned, the Chiefs scored another breakaway try and converted a penalty immediately after and they were suddenly 13 points in front.

The reserves came on as planned and Xolile called the signal for 'fourteen' – two hands held up followed by four fingers.

"The fourteen is the most lethal but also the most dangerous new tactic the Lions have been practising," Allison told her family, "it's basically playing Sevens rugby with fourteen players. In Sevens there are very few set pieces – scrums or lineouts – and the teams worry little about where on the field the action takes place. They don't care if the passes are moving the team backward so long as they retain possession. The danger in fifteen man rugby is that you if you lose possession while playing fourteen there is no defensive structure behind the ball so that any turnover is almost always seven points worth. And the turnovers are hard to prevent because your team is scattered over the width of the rugby field."

"So what's the advantage to the attacking team then?" asked Mitch.

"The advantage is that the ball is moved from hand to hand inviting the opponents to come out of their defensive structure to tackle – and in that process gaps open up that one does not normally find in top flight rugby. So it's a potent attacking weapon, but a dangerous one from the point of defence. Just one mistake can mean a huge points turn over."

Allison also said that although it was called 'fourteen' there were players who were stood down from the setup – namely the fullback, Jim had taken over from Xolile in this so that he could be the alternate playmaker – who remained the last line of defence. In addition there were two 'pillars' of tight forwards of two people each who remained just behind the half way line on the left and right. The idea was that if the opposing team pressured the passing game, the man with the ball could link up with one of these pods to make a ruck and begin the fourteen again.

With no scrums or line outs, the game moves quickly in the fourteen, Allison realised. The crowd seemed puzzled as the Lions moved the ball not only from side to side to side but often backwards as well. At one point Xolile was passed the ball only metres from his own tryline and he and Jeremy proceeded to work one-two passes back and forth until Jeremy was finally put down near the pod on the halfway line. When the ball was recycled, Jim took off, went between the fractured defence in the centre, and scored under the post.

Sixty seconds later the Chiefs had replied with a turnover and spectacular long range try of their own, but the conversion was wayward.

In the final ten minutes, the Lions continued the fourteen and with the advantage of three match winning backs, Xolile, Jim and the revitalised Sarel Prinsloo, the Lions scored two more tries. Both converted to run out not only winners but their third four try bonus in a row.

"Phew, that was nail biting," said Mitch. "Is this a vindication of the fourteen tactic?"

"Xolile believes that these surprise moves are not match winners in themselves but are variations that can throw opposing teams off their prepared moves. So one might not see the fourteen again for several weeks, or even not again this season."

63

"Dagger, tell us about the last manoeuvre, the one you call the fourteen. You are not going to try and make us believe it wasn't a rehearsed move, are you?"

"No, of course we've been practising that one... We have no secrets about this manoeuvre, it's simply the application of sevens rugby to the fifteen man game. And it is no secret, we actually invite other teams to play this sort of game against us – thirty players on the field all playing sevens should ensure spectacular play."

"Two games on tour, ten points in the bag. You are on a roll now, as a team?"

"We are absolutely – but in this competition you are only as good as your last game. We won today but we could very easily not win again this season. We saw at the start of the competition how easy it is to play ok but win nothing – anything can happen in the future."

"Next game against the Waratahs in Sydney. More fourteen tactic there too?"

"Perhaps; we'll have to see on the day how we feel, how their defence looks, a few other variables."

"Good luck with that game then."

64

On Skype Xolile confessed to Allison that the coming game against the Waratahs was proving to be extremely divisive for the team. Broadly the team was in two camps – the one headed by Willie believed that for the tour as a whole to be a success the Lions needed to 'throw' the game against the Waratahs by playing the second team; while a faction headed by Andile argued that one always put the best team on the park, always aimed to win every match "Otherwise why play?" he said.

Xolile was undecided but felt that he should support Willie, in the first instance. He told Allison that playing with the media was a game that ran in two directions – to dish it one also had to eat it sometimes – but he had seldom been as furious as when he read a local Australian newspaper that described Willie as a marionette dancing on the Dagger's string. He also thought if he stood down it would be a good time for Andile to captain the side. Eventually the matter was resolved with another vote on the team. This time the result was not nearly as clear cut as before the tour. The second string won out on the vote but narrowly. There were also several ties that Willie used his casting vote to push the second team members forward.

The Sydney newspapers were not kind to the selection. They called it a gesture of contempt and urged the Waratahs to punish the choices by the Lions management by putting fifty points on them come Saturday.

Xolile tweeted: *storm about nothing; nobody complains when Carter and McCaw are rested.*

The controversy was good for the gate though. A big crowd of nearly

30,000 pitched up, including a vocal branch of the Gay and Lesbian Coalition for the Lions. Xolile, on the bench as Willie wished, went around to talk with them. Phone numbers were exchanged and Xolile promised to bring the team around to a recommended gender bending bar next time they were in town.

With thirty minutes to go the result seemed to be as predicted. The Waratahs were fifteen points ahead and the drives by their big forwards were beginning to cross the advantage line regularly. At one point the number eight knocked the ball on, it was swooped on by Spickles as the Australian team waited for a whistle for a scrum. Spickles made a ten metre dart and as he was tackled offloaded to Jim on the inside. Jim pinned his ears back and found space that didn't seem to exist a moment before. Under ten seconds later he was dotting the ball down with his trade mark swan dive under the posts. The conversion was a formality.

"We're only eight points behind with half an hour to go," said Willie. "We can still win this."

To mixed cheers and jeers, the Lions emptied their bench and Xolile, Jeremy, Snake, Chimmy, Killer and two fresh loose forwards joined the team. Almost immediately the Lions won a breakdown penalty and Jeremy made to kick to set up a line out near the goal line. "Uh uh," said Xolile, "can you get it over the polls from here?"

"OK, boss," he said and duly added three more points.

Two scrum penalties followed versus a drop goal from the Waratahs and the teams entered the final five minutes with the Waratahs two points ahead. Xolile called 'moustache – Sandton' and the Lions went into slow, grind it up mode.

The Waratahs held off in the tackles so the Lions were able to make slow progress up field. The final whistle went and still the Lions held on to possession, ruck after ruck after ruck. It was a full three minutes after full time before the ref penalised the Sydney team for off side.

With the local crowd booing heartily, Jeremy slotted the routine penalty and, against everyone's predictions, including their own, the Lions won their third game on tour.

65

"Dagger, another game another victory – everything seems to be going right for the Lions at the moment."

"Yeah, Lionel, we were perhaps a bit lucky today so I would like to apologise to Sydney fans. We like to play adventurous rugby and succeed but the Waratahs were simply too strong today and we had to scramble the ugly win you all saw. If we meet in the playoffs we promise we'll play with more sparkle..."

"Still a win is a win and with 13 points from three games and one to play you're on target for a record haul from your Australasian tour. Is this what you expected?"

"Oh, yes, Lionel, we always thought we'd do well on tour but of course the season is a long way from being decided..."

As the players headed for the ice baths the captain of the day, Andile bellowed at them: "An unexpected victory can mean only one thing: tonight we drink."

66

The Lions flew into Perth from Hamilton the morning of the match against the Western Force. Traditionally Perth with its high incidence of South African and Zimbabwean émigrés was more friendly to rugby teams visiting from South Africa but the team was astonished to find themselves minor celebrities. There was a group of supporters at the airport and a small group of fans even sang along during the war cry. Once the game started more than once did the Australian commentators refer to the quite raucous support in the stadium for the Lions.

"Almost as good as a home match," said one.

"Probably more support for the Lions here than when they drive 60 kilometres from their homes to Pretoria to play the Bulls," said the other.

The Lions were well in control when ten minutes from the end Chimmy went off the field with a scalp gash. To some amusement from the crowd, Tsego came rolling on for his first Super Rugby cap.

Xolile slapped palms with him. "Ten minutes," he told him, "don't do anything rash, just hold up the scrum and keep your defensive line."

"Dagger," said the big man, "this is my first cap, it means so much to me. I'll never forget this moment...."

There was only one scrum in the last ten minutes and both sets of front ranks had little heart for a contest so Tsego was able to hold his end of the scrum up proficiently. But rugby is a funny game and in the last minute, probably because he couldn't keep up with the rucks, Tsego found himself out on the wing only twenty metres from the

Forces' tryline. Jim was holding up two tacklers, looking around for someone to pass to. He saw Tsego and sent a long looping pass to him. Amazingly Tsego took the ball like a wing. He clasped it to his chest and set off the corner flag. The cover defence of the Force charged across to cut him off. Many in the Lions team had stopped playing and were watching the tableau unfold as he pounded his gigantic legs into the turf, chest heaving, sweat flying off his face like a boxer…

He told Willie later that he had tried to shift the ball from his right arm to the left so he could fend off the tacklers but it appeared in the cruel gaze of the TV camera that with the line at his mercy he had simply bounced the ball out of his arms. The ball skittered away for a knock on as the tacklers brought him down. Tsego banged the grass with his hand so hard in frustration that the earth shook. The Force fans greeted his rising to his feet with derisive laughter.

Despite the spoiled try, in a result more about confidence and relaxation than anything else, the Lions ripped up their opponents, winning by seven tries to one.

Back in the change room, Tsego was still reliving his moment of agony. "Will I get another chance?" he asked Xolile.

"Who knows? You realise that fitness is your limitation? You need to keep working on that and you could become a regular. But to be honest you are still too fat to play regularly at this level." Xolile didn't see the need to sweeten the pill.

Tsego nodded as though no one had ever said that to him before. "I'll keep training" he promised.

A crowd of over 1,000 greeted the Lions at Johannesburg airport on their arrival from Australasia. With 19 points from a possible 20 on their overseas trip the Lions had leapfrogged into second position on the log and, with a brace of home games ahead, were now established as one of the favourites for the title.

Among the thousand was Allison and daughters. Andile swung her off her feet in a bear hug. Jeremy slapped palms with her and several of the team greeted her warmly.

Xolile and Allison stood suddenly face to face in the airport arrivals hall.

They made as if to embrace, almost shook hands and ended up staring into each others faces with silly grins.

"I say get a hotel room and be done with it," said Andile impishly before drawing them into a vigorous collective hug.

67

July 3rd 2015

The Lions vs The Crusaders

Venue: Ellis Park Stadium, Johannesburg

Weather: fine and mild, 15°C, breeze less than 5 km per hour from south to north

Crowd: 43,566

Result: Lions 22 Crusaders 16

Scorers:

Lions: tries 2 (Jason Swartz, Jim Mahlangu); penalties 2, conversions 2 (Jeremy Gandolfini)

Crusaders: tries 1 (Kelly McNamara); penalties 3, conversion 1 (Joe Smith)

Points: Lions 4, Crusaders 1

Jason had asked to see Xolile.

"Where's Chris?" Xolile asked him, unused to meeting him alone.

"No, it's just me, Dagger…"

Jason seemed to take a long run up to say something important. He used the word 'Dagger' in every sentence perhaps to cover his anxiety or perhaps as ongoing expression of respect.

"You know I don't want to worry the Dagger but I need to talk to the Dagger, very important. I know the Dagger is a busy man…" and so on.

Xolile refrained from looking at his watch but it was almost five minutes before an email printout was produced and Xolile learnt that Jason had a job offer from Munster.

"Look at the salary" he said to Xolile, and, indeed, it many times what either of them was earning at the Lions.

"I know you've said the team is everything but we're a poor family: this money is more than all my relatives have ever earned in their whole lives. For my nephews and nieces and cousins this is like a new life for all of them. They can go to Kimberley and study get decent jobs. It's … it's a miracle…"

Xolile bit back his first response. What he wanted to say, he confided to Allison later, was: you little shit, I found you, trained you, turned you into a star and now with not even one season in Joburg you want to take a high paid job in Ireland!

But he didn't. Instead he said: "Snake, I understand entirely. This must be like an early Christmas for all of you. But I want you to think of something else – you're still young, and unless you get a major injury, have a long career ahead of you. If you don't make the Springbok team this year then you should get there next. Then you'll be an established star who can command a big salary anywhere in

Europe or even in Durban or Pretoria. I understand your family is suffering but if they can wait a year or maximum two there should be even more money to lift them up forever."

Snake was nodding vigorously. "Chris said the same. He said the uselesses can wait or make their own arrangements."

Xolile decided to cut this short immediately. "Good. So don't leave for Ireland before we've won the Super 15, OK?"

"Yes, Dagger. Yes, thank you for the Dagger's time…"

68

In a surprise development, the Lions rugby team won second prize in a "Community Builders of the Year" competition. Sited as a major lever for the upgrading of disabled children's schools in three countries, Neil Gouws took the award on behalf of the team and delivered a very articulate speech about special needs and integration into the labour force.

"Amazing," commented Andile, "I've played with him for three years and never heard him string three words together, still less in English..."

Xolile had a minor sprain to his ankle and was stood down for the next match, against the Rebels from Melbourne. Dlamini invited him to view the game from the manager's box while they 'chatted about the future', according to him.

The two of them walked out in to the open area of the box just before kickoff. Ellis Park was close to full.

"Fifty four thousand tickets sold so far" said Dlamini, "and it looks to me as though there are thirty thousand black fans here."

"You should have distributed the unsold tickets to Soweto schools," said Xolile.

"Rubbish!" replied Dlamini, "we don't give away tickets when we're nearly sold out. We might give them away when we have an empty stadium but not when we can hope to be full at the next match.

"Dagger, I've got to say it: you've done it. No matter what happens from here the Lions are changed forever. We're planning to host the semi and the final, if you make it, at Soccer City."

Soccer City was the purpose built massive stadium built on the other side of Johannesburg for the 2010 Soccer World Cup final. Seating almost 90,000 spectators it was too big to be used much. Like almost all world cup stadia in South Africa, Soccer City was a white elephant with no anchor tenant and rising maintenance costs for the city.

"That's a good idea. But if money is the thing I thought you'd want to stay at the stadium you own?"

Dlamini slapped his shoulder with a chuckle. "Not if the city is going to rent Soccer City to us for next to nothing. Then we'll turn Ellis Park into Fan Parks for the last two games and rent it out next season to a football club. Neat, huh?"

The teams filed out on to the field. The public address system played Sobashiya and a fair number of the crowd sang along.

Dlamini nodded appreciatively. "You know I'm negotiating with Rihanna to sing Sobashiya if you guys make the final. That'll be something hey?"

"Yeah, something all right..."

"Tell the guys to sign no contracts with the French or the Brits until we've had a chance to counter offer. Everyone in the main squad should earn almost twice what they've earned this year. Maybe you, Mahlangu and Gandolfini can get three times... You'll stay on right, even if you make the Springbok team?"

"Sure..." Xolile suddenly had a frisson, a sense of foreboding and he shivered as the shadow of a plane temporarily cut off his sunshine.

July 10th 2015

The Lions vs The Rebels

Venue: Ellis Park Stadium, Johannesburg

Weather: fine and mild, 18°C, no wind

Crowd: 55,908

Result: Lions 53 Rebels 6

Scorers:

Lions: tries 7 (Jim Mahlangu 3, Ernest van Heerden 2, Chimurenga Tongona, Jeremy Gandolfini); penalties 2, conversions 6 (Jeremy Gandolfini)

Rebels: Penalties 2 (Oswald Kelly)

Points: Lions 5, Rebels 0

PART FOUR

69

"A rugby foursome," said Andile. "Who would have thought?"

The four in question stood on Xolile's roof garden. He had barbecued some ostrich meat, Japanese style, and had just disappeared down to the kitchen for a second bottle of duty free French champagne. Allison, Andile and Jakes sat on his bench sipping the ends of the first bottle.

Andile had his arm around Jakes' shoulders in a proprietorial fashion and she responded, Allison noticed, surprisingly girlishly, nestling into his arms.

"I thought you didn't date rugby players. When did you guys become a couple?" she asked Jakes.

"I just said that to give me time to find the biggest one," said Jakes.

"Oh, a week or two," Andile answered, "but tonight is the first time we've come out in front of the Dagger."

"Would he care?" she asked.

"Not if it didn't affect the team," answered Jakes, "but you know with me being sort of a coach he might be worried about domestic conflict spilling over into the team environment." She shrugged. "Not that we'd change anything but it would be nice if he were supportive."

"Well we're not a couple," said Allison.

Andile watched Xolile mount the steps silently behind her. "Some of the guys are saying if you two don't catch a wake up we'll have to speak to your parents on Xolile's behalf. You know, slip them a cow or two to get things moving..."

"I don't think that will be necessary," said Xolile and, before anyone could ask him what he meant, the sky behind him exploded in a fireworks display of sudden dazzling intensity.

They oohed and ahed as the lights lit up the still, early spring Highveld evening, eventually Allison remembered that there was a Hindu festival that day.

"Isn't this amazing," said Jakes, "here we are the bosses of the Super 15, well, not me, really, but you guys: I feel like I'm in the presence of the masters of the universe..."

They all laughed.

"Do you believe the Lions are going to win the cup?" Allison asked her.

"I do. Mainly because they are winning while using only a few of the new tactics, winning in the face of bad luck and bad referees. Of course you can never predict rugby outcomes accurately but I can't see how they could lose...."

"Dlamini believes the same. He's offering big wage increases for the squad to stay on next year." Xolile opened the champagne with a pop and poured into everyone's glass.

The magical evening continued. As the fireworks died down suddenly Andile and Jakes stood up and departed with minimal salutations.

"They're sexually charged," said Xolile with a diffident smile. He and Allison looked at each other in silence for long moments.

"Kids with their father this weekend?" he asked.

"Yes." And then: "I'm ten years older than you…"

He laughed. "You know I read this week the average length of a relationship in Joburg is less than four years. So in four years' time if we were still together, you'd still be ten years older than me."

They chuckled away conspiratorially. Then he held out his hand, she took it, and they slowly descended the spiral staircase to the living quarters below.

70

Allison lay in his bed. She had snoozed briefly but was now wide awake. It wasn't so much that the sex had been fantastic – although it had been – but she had never had sex before where the object of her desires had been so … perfect.

She gazed across at Xolile. He lay rolled in a ball on one side of the bed, snoring gently, contained. His body would have been the delight of an anatomy student, she thought, every muscle, every sinew was outlined almost like a caricature of good health. She had been shy about her own body, apologising for her stretch marks and slack belly.

He had dismissed her concerns with a laugh. "I'm the professional athlete in this relationship. I like you not because you've got a perfect body but a perfect mind."

First light crept in through the windows and Allison had a sudden premonition that something was going to go wrong. She crawled out of bed and dressed silently. There was a croissant shop just downstairs from Xolile's apartment. She stole out and bought four for their breakfast, as well as her own newspaper, The Star. On the second page the headline was "Dagger to be announced Springbok captain this week". In the body of the article it claimed that an unnamed source in the Springbok training camp leaked the news that the Dagger as well as up to seven uncapped players in the Lions team would be added to the national squad convening in Bloemfontein for training in two weeks time. She smiled with pleasure to herself. No surprise, she thought, but with the national team one could never be sure.

The city was waking in the early morning. A truck stopped and dumped a bundle of The Times morning newspapers and she bought one from the vendor.

And the bottom dropped out of her world. The banner headline read: **"Dagger a drug kingpin and ex jail bird."**

71

Xolile was still sleeping when she got back inside.

"Hey!" she said none too gently and woke him with a nudge. He smiled affectionately at her and held out his arms.

"Look at these first" she told him and gave him the two newspapers. He read both articles quickly, stopped at The Times' story. "Oh no, not now, damn it all to hell!"

"What is it? It's true? Say it isn't so?" She was conscious of how high pitched and shrill her voice had become.

"Well, the drug kingpin bit is overstated but it is essentially accurate. This is what happened..."

Xolile spoke earnestly to Allison for the next hour, sometimes holding her hand, sometimes pacing around his flat. Allison sat for her part stony faced, then when he had finally wound down, surprised them both by bursting into tears.

"When were you going to tell me?" she asked.

"It is a secret, or it was until this morning. You can't keep a secret by telling it to people...."

"We've just slept together, you shit! Didn't it occur to you that there was a trust thing between us or did it just run in one direction, from me to you?"

He tried to reason with her, to tell how strong his feeling were for her but she would not listen and ten minutes later, still crying, she was in her car heading home.

Xolile sat in his lounge for many minutes after Allison had left. He fiddled with the Ntseku almost reflexly. Then suddenly he leapt to his feet and began to yell curses to the room in Japanese. He flung every vile and taboo curse he had picked up in his five years in a Japanese jail. Still bellowing the swear words he flung the Ntseku on the floor and jumped on it, grinding it almost to dust with his heels. He carried on screaming and jumping on the artefact until he stopped ten minutes later, soaked in sweat.

He stopped as suddenly as he had begun, gave a shake of his head and then fetched a little broom and a scoop from the kithchen. Almost reverentially he swept the remains of the Ntseku in to the scoop before pouring it into the bin.

"Reassume control" he told himself sternly.

72

The seminar room at Ellis Park was full, fifty people including the expanded squad and coaches and other support staff. A smattering of hesitant applause broke out as Xolile strode to the microphone. He spoke with a gentle diffidence, a whimsy almost.

Xolile's story:

I think all of you have seen today's newspapers. In short, other than portraying me as a mafia boss of major proportions, what they wrote is largely accurate.

I kept all these details a secret – even from Willie and Allison – I felt I had to in order to survive in the Lions. Allison is furious at me for not telling her, she feels I betrayed our friendship. I hope she'll get over it in time. But perhaps some of you are angry about it as well. I apologise and I maintain that I kept my past hidden only because I had no option.

I'm going to tell you my side of the story – these will be details I won't give the newspapers – and then I'm going speculate on what is going to happen to me and how it might impact on the team.

When I left school in the Transkei I drifted into Cape Town and started work at a night club in Sea Point, mostly cleaning, then a bit of admin and cashing later. I met a guy who said that I looked a likely lad to make some real money. I said that's me and he recruited me to be a drug mule, someone who transports drugs from one side of the world to another by hiding them in their clothes or bags. I did that for two years, more or less. I did it for the money, plain and simple, and by the time I was twenty one I had a few hundred thousand rand in my bank account.

As a mule I was very successful. I travelled as an African student with an offer to an American university or sometimes as a Kenyan runner going to train in Germany. I made dozens of trips on four passports. Then I started running my own mules and I made even more money. So when I made my last trip in to Japan I was just filling in for a young girl, one of my one stable of mules, if you like, who had developed appendicitis at the last moment.

Everything was fine initially but at Tokyo airport they were trying a new system – instead of searching based on suspicion they searched every seventeenth passenger going through customs. I was the seventeenth and I knew I was done for – I was carrying close to R50, 000 worth of heroin in my bags. As a last resort I tried to bribe the Japanese officials. I got an extra six months for that. I think I should say that I tried heroin and cocaine a couple of times each but drugs are not my thing, really. For me it was just a business.

So I stood trial in Japan and served eventually four and half years in Fukuoka jail in Northern Japan.

One has to understand how Japanese jails work – they are very different from South African ones. Gangs are big in Japanese prisons but they don't rule by violence much and stabbing people or killing others is pretty much unknown. They rule by influence both within and without the prison walls.

I was lucky that I shared a cell with someone who became a close friend. Yukio Moshimura is serving twenty years for defrauding thousands of pensioners in a pyramid scam. But his hobbies are Japanese language and culture and betting on sports matches.

Perhaps you can imagine what it was like when I showed up in his cell – I spoke no word of Japanese and he spoke no English. He couldn't pronounce my name so he called me 'Tawagoto heddo'. It was three months before I realised he was calling me shithead in Japanese.

But cell mates become intimates in a way that even husband and wife don't. Within a year my Japanese was fluent; within two years I could read and write it pretty well. Yukio persuaded me to play rugby in jail because he was betting on the outcomes of the prison league. The authorities had encouraged rugby, as well as boxing, karate and weight lifting, some ten years ago because they feared turning the prison gangs into US style drugs and weapons based groups. The belief was that contact sports provided an outlet for physical excesses.

So there was money available for the prison rugby league and if you were a player you could have certain privileges. For example when my prison team won the final two years ago we played in a University stadium in front of nearly ten thousand people. After the final I wandered out of the grounds and I suddenly realised that I was alone – there were no guards and no one knew where I was. Of course, as a foreigner in Japan I couldn't easily escape, and my time was nearly up anyway, so I caught a taxi back to the prison the next day.

I think I must admit to you, and I hope that this doesn't leak in to the newspapers, that Yukio and I made a lot of money betting on matches that I could influence. For example, I was averaging three tries every two matches. Yukio would bet, through an intermediary at another prison, on me scoring two tries in the first ten minutes of a match, say, against Tokyo central. Of course I couldn't be sure that I would score two tries in ten minutes but I would try and the odds favoured the bettor so we began to make a lot of money.

Allison accused me of having secret plans hatched over five years in a prison cell. That's not the case: rather I realised after a while that what I was doing pretty much full time, that is, looking for rugby talent, encouraging it in various ways, and playing myself, might be applicable back home when I left the jail. And the difficulties in Japan of putting fifteen players on the park every week were much larger than in Johannesburg. Often we'd go into a match in the prisons league with a player, or even two, who had never played rugby before. I'd play them a video of a Super match and one of them would say: yes, I think I can play scrumhalf.

So after five years I left the prison with a lot of friends, an interest in Japanese literature and culture and this tattoo on my body. I knew already that fullback was my position so I stopped off in Melbourne for six months and joined a junior Aussie rules club. And practiced taking the high ball, hour after hour, day after day. The rest of the time I hung around in coffee bars reading Japanese books.

Then I came to Johannesburg, met Willie and all of you.

So that's my secret past: any questions or comments before I turn to the future?

Chimmy put up his hand, all 117 kilograms of him according to the latest weigh ins. "You know, Dagger, I owe everything to you – without you I'd still be playing club rugby. But, according to my faith, trafficking in drugs is a major sin, enough to get you cast out in to the place of permanent suffering, a place where you can never return from, a place..."

"Get on with it" shouted Jeremy Gandolfini at him. "There's no point in telling us what your beliefs are – we've heard them a million times. What's done is done and there's no sense in your warning us about hell now."

Snake spoke from the back. "To me this is a nothing, this is history. We know why we play for the Lions – because we have issues or nobody else will play with us. Dagger, you'll always be welcome in our team..."

General agreement followed.

Xolile nodded warmly. "Unfortunately there are other agents involved, most notably the owners of the team. Nobody knows which way they are going to jump – maybe nothing happens, maybe they suspend me, maybe they fire me. They have all the power. If I can't play in the last two games we'll make do and still win. Charles van Wyk, you'll come in if necessary to replace me. After warming the bench the whole season you'll finally get a chance. Andile of course will be captain. And we go on, right?"

73

It was the last night before Xolile's release and he and Yukio were doing what they had done almost every night for the previous five years – they were practicing calligraphy. On a largish white board across the table in the centre of their cell they drew or wrote a series of large ideograms with small paint brushes. Usually Yukio went first and Xolile would copy. When they got to an ideogram he was unfamiliar with, Yukio would show him how to pronounce it, write it and the derivation.

As he had done almost every night, Xolile admired his own artwork. What precision, what grace, he told himself. Yukio, on the other hand, frequently told him he wrote like a clumsy child. It was several minutes before Xolile noticed that they were writing the same statement over and over again. They wrote in Japanese: my strength is my ability to know another man and to shape him to my will.

"Is this my will or yours?" Xolile said to him.

"Both," said Yukio, "but remember it's still eight years before I get a chance to bend anyone other than you to my will. And here is my last gift to you…" He handed him the little Ntseku with the rugby ball held to his stomach.

"Thank you," said Xolile gravely, "but what else have you given me?"

Yukio laughed. "I have taught you to speak the most beautiful of languages, yes, yes you have told me many times of your own language, the one with the primitive clicks, the language of poets, you claim. But, you know, to speak Japanese, even badly as you do, is a special gift…. And you know, Sho-li, I have taught you something more useful – to shape a man to your will, as we write it today, is a

227

skill you will use, must use, on the outside. This is your strength, much more so than running fast or being elusive. This is what will bring you success, perhaps even fame...."

Xolile nodded. "This is true; what you have taught me of Japanese language and culture has augmented me, has made me larger than before. Even though in five years you have still not done me the honour of learning my real name..."

They chuckled together. Xolile rubbed the Ntseku between his thumb and forefinger. "And in eight years then the world will see a thing or two," he said to Yukio.

"Indeed" said Yukio and poured them each a tiny glass of contraband saki.

74

Allison was waiting outside his apartment.

"You came back; I'm so pleased," he told her.

"I'm still damned annoyed at you. But I realised we need to release a statement so I came back to help you with it…"

"I wrote a draft months ago for just this eventuality. Come upstairs and let's see if we can use it."

"But tell me one thing: this is terrible for you, in effect all you've built might disappear completely in a few days – and yet you seem almost detached, almost as if it's happening to someone else…"

He nodded. "You know every day for the last 18 months just before I go to sleep I ask myself: what if it comes out tomorrow, what would I do, how would I feel? And every night I rehearse my responses, what would I say to the team, to you, to the fans? And then as I drift off, I believe that I'm comfortable that I can handle it, that it won't be too bad.

"So now that it has happened, the worst case scenario and more – I'm surprised at how much it hurts, how I've got this constant pain in the centre of my chest. The only thing that it reminds me of was when I was in love for the first time and my girlfriend Zanele told me she preferred my friend Jacob. Then I had this pain, just here, like heartburn but not sore…" he indicated the centre of his chest. "It lasted for four weeks I remember because it got better only when I left for Grahamstown. I don't know how long this one is going to last…"

"But you show absolutely no signs of distress!"

"I'll be damned if I show my pain to anyone." He began to nibble on her neck.

"Not even me? Stop it…" she was suddenly engulfed by indolence.

It was an hour or so before they had sated themselves and were able to review the statement.

It said simply: *I, Xolile Dalindyebo, served five years in a Japanese jail for heroin smuggling. I was guilty as charged, served my full sentence without remission and am now rehabilitated. I do not myself, consume drugs, never have in fact, and do not sell them to others nor encourage others to take drugs themselves.*

I have paid my debt to society in full and wish now to put this matter behind me.

Allison made a few changes and they released onto his facebook page. Within hours every newspaper in the country, and many across the rugby playing world, had reprinted it or summarised it.

"The twitter traffic around this is enormous," she told him.

"What's the general feeling?"

"Disbelief mostly. That's all going to change now that you acknowledge the charges."

"Can we use this against the bosses if they try and fire me?"

"Maybe… if the bosses even know what twitter is."

75

Willie and Xolile sat in James Dlamini's office. Coffee, brandy and cigars had been offered. The three of them sat around a little low table in front of his big desk. Dlamini was warm and friendly.

"Look," he said, "we've got to manage this carefully. Some members of my board, and, frankly, these are the most important members, take a very strong line against drugs. The Chairman of the Board, Nicholas White, lost a son to heroin about three years ago. He's a zealot about punishing drug smugglers. We've got to give things a chance to settle down. Dagger, I'd like you to stand down against the Waratahs in the semi finals. The team looks like it can win without you..."

"I won't do that" said Xolile firmly. "I'm the captain and I play until the coach doesn't select me."

"Come on, man. That's not a useful attitude. Willie, can you just not pick the Dagger for the rest of the campaign? Next year is another story, much of all this will be forgotten by then I'm sure..."

Willie shifted in his seat, cleared his throat a few times.

"Uh, Mr Dlamini, according to my contract, picking the team is my responsibility, which I do without management input or advice. That is how it has always been and that is how it will continue to be. I am not obliged to take selection restrictions from my employers..."

Dlamini turned ugly immediately. "Listen here, you couple of country bumpkins. Here is the Dagger's contract, signed by him and countersigned by both Willie and myself. Clause 31e says: have you ever been guilty of a criminal offence, no, yes, details. And there's the

Dagger's mark and signature right there next to no criminal offences. This is a dismissible omission – you've lied on your contract with the Lions."

"Then you must dismiss me. But I'm not firing myself. I believe I've have done nothing currently wrong and I see no reason to withdraw merely to make the public relations easier for the franchise." Xolile sipped his brandy with an air of nonchalance.

"And the same must apply for me," said Willie. "I can't drop a player on management's request. But if he is no longer eligible for selection through a disciplinary procedure then I have no choice, of course."

"The board is simply going to insist that the Dagger doesn't play. If you won't stand down, for the good of the team, for yourselves, for the future, I'll be forced to dismiss you. Then nobody wins, certainly not me..."

"Let us meet with the board, speak to them, try and show them our point of view," said Xolile.

Dlamini argued with them for several more minutes, but, failing any other way forward, agreed to put their request for a meeting with the board in front of the chairman.

"I don't think we can win this one," said Willie as they left the building.

76

Meanwhile the twitter storm raged on. According to Allison, the tweets were divided roughly fifty fifty between support and criticism of Xolile. Much of the criticism was of the yes-but –he-should-have variety, with comparatively few calling for Xolile's head, or in this case, his suspension or dismissal.

Allison tried to find unusual viewpoints to show Xolile.

If he could win us the Super Rugby cup I'd have Charles Manson as captain, wrote Cynthia van Staden.

The Dagger is the greatest Lion since Kobus Wiese. Leave him alone, wrote Karel Cupido.

The Dagger supported Andie Macdonald when he was bust for cocaine; he's soft on drug use, wrote Truthtopower.

The Dagger is Satan's emissary; his weapons are drugs for sale, wrote Biblelover

"There are a few people who commented similarly. They say if you don't encourage others to take drugs, as you say, why did you rush to defend a convicted drug taker like Macdonald?"

"That might have been a mistake to comment on his case. Overconfidence probably on my part," answered Xolile.

"Would you like to respond, try and set the record straight?"

"Nah, I think I should keep quiet unless I have something really good to add. Is there any way we can intervene in this or do we have to just let the voices of the people drone on?"

"Well I've been thinking... " Xolile started stroking her arm and she paused, momentarily distracted. "I've been thinking that we could set up a twitter vote: should The Dagger be dismissed or not? A simple yes or no vote..."

"And what would that achieve?"

"It might add pressure to the Board's decision, make them believe that they would face a fan revolt if they acted against you."

"But what if I lose the vote?"

"Then you say the churches and mosques got their members to block vote against you, that the results were fixed."

They chuckled away together. "OK," he said eventually, "Do it."

77

The board meeting was surprisingly low key to Willie and Xolile. The chairman, Nicholas White and seven others were present. White, a grey haired man in his sixties did most of the talking.

"Mr Dalindyebo, thank you for coming with the coach. We are all collectively in admiration for what you have done individually and as a leader of the Lions. We are anxious to hear your justification for continuing to be employed by the Lions. At the end of that the board will take a free vote as to whether you should be dismissed on the grounds of hiding your criminal record at the time of your recruitment.

"I know that some of the board, notably James Dlamini, will argue on your behalf while I will, unless you can persuade me otherwise, lead the charge of those who seek your exclusion. Is that a fair summary of the process this afternoon? Everybody in agreement? James? Let us proceed then."

Xolile opened his mouth to speak but White wasn't done yet. "I will say, because I imagine you have done your homework on this anyway, that my son, Russell, died of a heroin overdose in Amsterdam three years ago. So I have strong feelings about drug smugglers, as you can imagine."

Once again Xolile opened his mouth to begin his defence but this time it was Willie who spoke.

"My cousin had an adult son who committed suicide a while back, hanged himself in the garage. It was terrible for the whole family but particularly for my cousin, Ernst. He blamed himself, kept on rehashing the early years, the time he beat his son for lying, the time he missed his prize giving at school, the time he lashed out at his wife in front of the boy. Even today he still hasn't fully recovered. A month ago he spent the whole afternoon telling me of the holiday he and the boy took when he was fifteen. But nothing gives him any comfort..."

Nicholas White nodded respectfully at this speech and seemed to encourage Willie with little bobs of his head. But Willie seemed to have run out of steam.

"Your point being?" White asked eventually in a gentle tone.

Willie seemed nonplussed. If he had a point when he started speaking he seemed now to have lost it. As he ummed and ahhed, Xolile broke in: "I think the point is that Willie's cousin didn't blame the rope."

The room was silent for long seconds. White rubbed his hand across his face and when he finally spoke he sounded old and tired. "So you're saying that when a child dies there is a kind of madness that grips the parents, that they are so overcome with grief and guilt they grab at anything in search for an explanation; that in my case I am so wracked that I am pursuing a talented sportsman, equivalent to a rope for a hanged man, for a smuggling crime that he has already paid in full for, rather than looking at my own role in his death. Yes?"

"Put better than I could, Sir," said Willie.

"It certainly is a viewpoint," said White, "but it is not one I share. I regard drug smuggling as similar to, but not as serious as, murder. The way to discourage murder, and hard drug smuggling, is to punish these crimes with all the means society has at its disposal. To discourage others from doing it at every level in society so that only the most desperate and contemptible individuals would ever consider these crimes as options. That's my view. Mr Dalindyebo," he gave Xolile a polite smile, "let's hear your justification."

Xolile's turn was essentially around two points that Allison had given him the previous night. Firstly, that a principle in Western law was that people should not be punished twice for the same crime. He, Xolile, had already been punished once in jail in Japan and if he were to be fired now this would constitute a second penalty.

The other argument was that if society decided that no one could be rehabilitated then all jail terms were in effect life sentences – no one could resume their place in society after jail. With no rehabilitation possible criminals would become even more desperate to avoid jail, would in effect adopt a 'you won't take me alive' position, to the detriment of police and the whole legal system.

At the end of the afternoon White surprised both of them by saying that the board's decision would be communicated to them on Monday of the next week. Xolile was free to play in the semi final, at least.

As they walked out Xolile put his hand on Willie's shoulder. "You are a good man, Willie. I think people often don't give you the credit you deserve."

"Oh fuck off," said the coach shyly.

78

The semi final of the Super 15 rugby competition took place at The Calabash, the site of the 2010 Soccer World Cup Final. It was contested by the Waratahs from Sydney and the Lions from Johannesburg in front of 80,000 spectators.

Joburg was awash with excitement and preparations for the match. There were fan parks where people who couldn't or wouldn't go to the match could watch it on a giant screen while drinking themselves into a stupor. The biggest of them were at Ellis Park itself, Melrose Arch for the wealthy and Orlando in Soweto for the new black fans.

The stadium itself shimmered in the late afternoon heat. Five hundred buses were pressed into service from six park and ride sites around the city while vendors did a roaring trade both at the bus sites and the roads leading up to the stadium. Amongst the fans almost ten thousand foreigners, most from Sydney, added to the money flowing into the city.

And for once, a big rugby match had a strong black presence among the spectators. Andile and Xolile argued about the percentage – Andile said sixty and Xolile forty five - but no one could deny that this was an unprecedented event.

As the TV commentator put it: "In ten years time or less we could see rugby becoming the number one sport amongst all races in South Africa."

When the time for the war cry came the whole concrete stadium shook as the crowd stamped their feet and bellowed the refrain. Newspapers later compared it to the crowd that greeted the first of the Robben Islanders released by apartheid in the late eighties.

In the face of all this hype and glitz it should have been no surprise that the rugby wasn't great. Both teams seemed to suffer an acute attack of nerves and passes were dropped all over the stadium for the duration of the match. The one exception was Xolile himself.

As he put it to Allison: "This could be my last Lions match for a long period, or even forever. Or worst of all, this might be my last top flight rugby match. I'm planning to go out with a bang."

When he ran on to the field the boos and catcalls were substantial but seemed to be outweighed by cheers.

And certainly there were no boos when he scored a try – which he did three times in the first half. He scored his first try after a prolonged series of forward drives close to the line. The ball seemed to be stuck in a ruck but he saw it, plucked it out and put it down over the tryline in one movement. He scored his second when he received a javelin throw from Clubman. He then broke through the Waratahs' defence, passed and received the last pass back from Jim.

The third came on the dot of half time. The Lions were playing the Park Station moustache manoeuvre with everyone up playing at high tempo. At one point the ball was turned over close to the Waratahs twenty two metre line and almost in desperation the Aussie fly half hacked the ball straight down the middle of the field. Xolile was on his own twenty two when he hauled the ball in. He turned and faced the ideal position for him : the Waratahs' defensive line was fractured, with some chasing the high ball, some still hanging off the ruck fifty metres back, and some just lying about in exhaustion.

Allison called it immediately in the stadium. "They'll never catch him now, that's seven points," she told her daughters. And she was right as Xolile simply ran through the opposing team. He jinked left then right; he changed his pace, sometimes breathtakingly fast, sometimes just holding the ball as though waiting for support. He dummied, made as if to pass to Jim coming up fast on his inside and then in a single burst of acceleration beat the last of the Australian defenders to score under the post.

As the half time hooter sounded he trotted back to his position to the sound of many thousands of people chanting "Dagger! Dagger! Dagger!", the sound merging into one so it sounded like a giant wave. Allison burst into tears, alarming her family. "I'm fine. Just leave me alone for a while," she said.

Ten minutes after half time, as agreed before the match, Xolile was replaced by Charles van Wyk. Everyone had agreed he needed the game time in case he had to play the final the next week.

Xolile left the field to resounding applause. The Waratahs came back strongly in the third quarter but by the time the last ten minutes rolled around the altitude caught up with them and they faded badly. The Lions won by 12 points and the gigantic crowd went home happy.

79

On the Tuesday after the match, as the city at once seemed to glorify in the won semi final and prepare itself for the bigger one, the final, only four days away, the news broke that the Lions board had fired Xolile, ostensibly for lying on his contract about a history of imprisonment. Not only did they fire him but sought and obtained a court injunction that prevented him from coming within one hundred metres of the Lions, their change rooms, or their training field. In effect, it meant he could not even attend the final and certainly could not act as the water boy as he and Willie had planned.

Willie had warned the team that this was on the cards so there were no surprises there. But no one expected the twitter fury that overtook the ether. Before his banning the audience had been divided about his future, with the vote 56 to 44 percent critical of him. Now the posts were overwhelming in support of him. Waverers who previously had called for his head now howled not only at the firing but also at the seeming pettiness of the restriction order. The volume of votes quadrupled overnight and now the results were 70 percent in favour of Xolile.

And now a collective madness seemed to take over the twitter waves. Individuals called for increasingly outlandish resolutions – and seemed to find a thread of support for the craziest of them.

Xolile was making Tepinyaki for the magnificent seven plus Allison on his apartment patio. At the urging of the players, Allison began to scan the twitter waves for what was new.

Firstly, *PDoff* of Witbank called for a boycott of the final. Several messages of support flowed in for him until someone reminded him that the tickets were already sold out.

TMalaka wrote: *there's a very strong chance that an urgent injunction to the Supreme Court would result in interim relief in making the Dagger available for the final*

Then *Fransman* suggested a protest rally outside the Lions management offices at Ellis Park on the Wednesday afternoon. In response *Iknowmygod* asked others to join him in a counter rally supporting the firing of the Dagger.

"Oh no!" said Allison, "there could be bloodshed between the two groups."

"Dagger, now's your chance. Lead the march to the Provincial government and take over the country. You can be the new Castro." Jeremy Gandolfini had arrived sporting an engagement ring. ("Who's the groom?" Killer had asked.)

"And I can appoint you Minister of Crazy Ideas, right?" Xolile answered as he opened another bottle of Saki.

Andile was completely unimpressed. "Rugby fans? Rallying in the middle of the week with no beer on hand? I can promise you no one will pitch up for either group."

In the event he was completely correct. On the appointed afternoon a couple of dozen people arrived, most of them the curious rather than the outraged, wandered around for a while and then went home.

But it was JLouw of Roodepoort, an old twitter user, who really stirred things up. He wrote: *What's up with the rest of the Lions? Why don't they go on strike until the Dagger is reinstated?*

Over a hundred messages of support for this criticism followed, including some that called the team cowardly and failing to support their captain and mentor.

"They're right," said Snake, "we're just spectators in this, we need to take the fight to the Lions management." A couple of others nodded in agreement.

Allison afterwards said that this was just about the only time she had seen Xolile angry.

"Don't be idiots!" he said. "What are we aiming to do this year? Keep me in the team? No. Our aim is win the title and instil new support, new tactics, new songs, new attitudes – I could go on and on. We are certainly not looking to sacrifice all that for a minor dispute with our bosses. Andile, you're captain now, make sure everyone on the team understands that. If the twittering classes accuse us of this or that we keep silent, we don't follow every hair brained scheme that someone with a smart phone thinks up. I'll do my best to put these ideas to rest. Allison we need to draft a reply tonight..."

80

From the facebook page of Xolile Dalindyebo:

Since my firing by the Lions many people have offered advice and support. To all of you my heartfelt thanks. However some things need to be said loud and clearly:

1. The aim of the team is to win the cup. They cannot be disturbed by what is, in the end, a minor dispute between myself and the management.
2. Calls for the team to do something about this dispute are inappropriate. The team has no role in the dispute.
3. The dispute in any event has probably run its course. I am not going to pursue a legal option to secure my reinstatement, nor is any appeal process being contemplated.
4. Several other offers have come in for my employment in the new year and consequently I am flying to Japan on the day of the match to consult with some potential new employers.
5. I would suggest that any supporters I do have, can demonstrate their seriousness by making sure the Lions are as fully supported as possible at the final on Saturday.

81

On the Thursday afternoon before the final, Andile took the team through the 'Captain's run', a training period when he was effectively in charge, at the University of Johannesburg rugby ground. They rehearsed their set pieces, scrums, lineouts and kick offs, where every individual knew his role, as well as the five special techniques evolved during the year – the javelin, moustache Sandton and moustache Park Station, the chicken wing and the fourteen.

Fairly content with the collective performances, he lead the team into the change room only to find a black man in an overall, balaclava and scarf pacing around impatiently.

"Ah!" said Andile, "the Black Pimpernel is in the house."

Xolile flung aside his balaclava and scarf as players clustered around him and greeted him with various handshakes, embraces and punches. "I don't have much time. The guards recognised me when I came in they are on their walkie talkies to the supervisor or someone as we speak."

He assumed his familiar position in the centre of the room and began:

"I leave on Friday night for Japan so you will definitely be on your own for the final. I won't even know the result until I land, probably. I know the coaches and Andile will have last minute things to tell you but I felt I needed to say goodbye and tell you my opinion of the tactics for the match.

"Firstly, the obvious: you the greatest team in the world, ever, with no exceptions or reservations. I hope I'll play with you all again in the future but that is unknown.

"As far as tactics go, I want to suggest to you that you forget that this is a final, the biggest match in all your careers so far. Rather remember that you are playing for the 90,000 in the stadium and the millions around Joburg, many of whom have never watched a game of rugby before in their lives. They, the new fans, would like you to win but will support you, even if you lose on Saturday.

"But if you want to convert them and their families to rugby you need to play a game that thrills them, that keeps them on the edge of their seats, that in effect, makes them think that soccer is boring by comparison. And to do that you can't grind out a win against the Crusaders – you've got to take the game to them and provide a game in a thousand for the fans..."

There was a loud banging on the swing doors to the change room. "That's probably my police escort out of here," said Xolile, "so I'll end there – remember these are just my opinions, you are free to accept or reject them as you wish. Goodbye and good luck."

He stepped away but before he could leave, Andile pushed the doors open and put his large body in the way of the security guards. Then each individual embraced Xolile, some, like the Snake, having to be prised off him.

82

Allison and Xolile stood at the entrance to the Gautrain station, the railway from central Johannesburg to the airport.

"Last tally: two offers from France, firm at a salary that made me gasp. Interest from Saracens and, this might even stimulate your curiosity, a low pay but total control offer from the Griffons in Welkom – they want you to guide the team back into the Currie Cup premier league."

"I think Japan is my first choice but you have to go there to do deals, that's how it is. And you'll think about the girls and you coming over if I land a big one? Good English language schools there plus learning Japanese will give them an advantage in their careers, no matter what they plan to do."

"Oh just shut up about Japan already," said Allison and embraced him fiercely. "You know I'm unlikely to be able to leave before the girls finish school – and that's in four years' time."

They shared a long kiss.

"And in four year's time…" Allison went on "I'll still be ten years older than you!" they both finished the sentence laughing in the shared warmth.

They embraced once more and then he was gone.

83

At Tokyo airport, Xolile bought the Asahi Shimbun newspaper with great joy. He loved reading Japanese newspapers. He turned to the sports page.

The article was headed: *Lions from Johannesburg win Super 15 in a champagne performance against the Crusaders from Christchurch by seven tries to five.*

And then later: storm erupts around Lions captain post match comments. Andile Phike, straight after the victory said: "First I'd like to say that this win would only have been possible with the help of the Almighty – the Almighty Xolile Dalindyebo, the world's greatest rugby player."

Blasphemy accusations followed the captain's comments, according to the newspaper, with several churches calling for his disciplining.

Xolile's laugh boomed out across the airport.

THE END

POSTSCRIPT

The Japanese city of Honshu is a mixed industrial and university town. Yasunobu Kobayashi pushed open the swing doors to the noodle bar, enjoying the sudden steamy warmth after the freezing weather outside.

He ordered a bowl of noodles and took it to sit at a row of benches half occupied by men in thick jackets. He did a double take when he saw a black man sitting on one end of the benches. He went over.

"Excuse me," he said in Japanese, "but I know you, don't I? I've seen you on TV."

The man smiled and shook his hand. "Ah, you are a rugby fan. Who are you?" he said.

"I am Yasunobu Kobayashi. I study engineering at the University and play rugby for the second team. I play centre."

"Aha" said the stranger encouragingly.

"My dream is to make the first team, hopefully next year, before I graduate. What are you doing here in Honshu?"

The man picked up a grain of rice with his chopsticks. "I am looking" he said "for the Seven Samurai…"

MUSIC

The liberation song, Sobashiya Abazali Ekhaya , can be found at: http://www.last.fm/music/Amandla+Group/_/Sobashiya+Abazali+Ekh aya